Wedding Bell Blues

Other Avalon Books by Alice Sharpe

Wedding Bell Blues

ALICE SHARPE

AVALON BOOKS
THOMAS BOUREGY AND COMPANY, INC.
401 LAFAYETTE STREET
NEW YORK, NEW YORK 10003

PRINTED IN THE UNITED STATES OF AMERICA
ON ACID-FREE PAPER
BY HADDON CRAFTSMEN, SCRANTON, PENNSYLVANIA

This book is dedicated to my favorite
sister, Mary Shumate.

I'd like to offer my grateful acknowledgement to
Donna Stevens, a bridal consultant who truly loves
her work, and to the Sunny Brae Animal Clinic,
especially Jerry Ross, AHT.

Chapter One

I was old enough to know that there are some things a person should never admit to another person, especially a stranger. For me, the biggie was that I hated weddings. Having a big mouth and an even bigger imagination, I couldn't even leave it at that. I had to add, ''I hate frilly white dresses and miniature rosebuds and champagne punch and tuxedos and photographers and garters—''

''Whoa there!'' the person to whom I was confessing this said. Her name was Michelle Green, and I had met her only a few hours before. ''Wait a sec, Kylie,'' she added.

But I was on a roll. ''I hate confetti and those little lace-wrapped bundles of rice, or now, for the environmentally conscious, birdseed. I hate diamonds and organdy and flower girls and veils and those three-

1

tiered cakes with the little bride and groom standing on top, and—''

''I'm confused,'' Michelle said, interrupting me again, but I was beginning to run out of steam, so this time I took a deep breath and another swallow of champagne, which I really didn't like but it was my brother Matt's wedding and he'd handed it to me, so I had to drink it, right? Wrong, I decided and set the glass down on the table beside me.

''What are you confused about?'' I asked Michelle. Like I said, we'd just met—she was the girlfriend of the drummer in the band my brother had hired to play at the reception. She was in her mid-twenties, like me, and we'd just started talking about this and that when she'd said, ''Don't you love weddings?''

I'd been about to offer my usual evasive answer when I looked into her eyes and saw they'd gone all misty as she gathered in the visual images of my new sister-in-law in her white gown and Matt in his tux. Something had snapped, and I'd begun my tirade.

''Didn't you just tell me you're a bridal consultant at Barton's Department Store?'' Michelle asked.

''Oh, that.''

''But you hate weddings?''

I nodded.

''Isn't that kind of a . . . contradiction?''

That was an understatement. Bridal consultants are supposed to love weddings. After all, we dress the bride and her attendants, and what's not to love—

except for the few things I'd mentioned and the dozen I hadn't, none of which had to do with Johnny Page and the most humiliating experience of my life. I said, "Forget I said any of this."

"Hm—" she said, her eyes filled with curiosity.

"No, really, one sip of champagne, and I babble on like an idiot." Idiot was right. Self-preservation—job-wise—began to seem more important than being excruciatingly honest with a stranger.

"You were just telling it like you see it," Michelle said. "I think it's funny, but I still don't see how you can hold the job you have, feeling the way you do—"

"No, it was just a joke. Gosh, doesn't my brother look happy!" I said, hoping to divert her attention. She followed my lead and my gaze. Matt looked as splendid in his black tuxedo as any groom ever had; in fact, with his dark hair and eyes, he looked like a star from one of those old forties movies. Sandy, his bride, was resplendent in the pristine white dress I'd helped her choose, right down to the satin pumps decorated with tiny seed pearls.

Her six bridesmaids, all dressed up in long dresses of peach organdy, were clustered behind her. I'd had to talk fast to avoid ending up as part of the wedding party, but eventually Sandy had believed me when I said I would be way too busy organizing her wedding to participate in it. The fact was that dressing in those full-skirted bridesmaids' dresses always made me feel like an extra on the set of *Gone With The Wind* as well as a first-class phony.

Matt saw me staring and grinned at me. For one second my resolve wavered. For one second he looked so happy and so hopeful that I almost believed he and Sandy would beat the odds and have a long, happy life together. But isn't that what everyone thinks at a wedding?

Michelle said, ''He's cute, you know?''

''Very,'' I agreed and returned my gaze to her. She was an attractive woman who looked alluring in her green dress, with her fair hair piled atop her head. She was the kind of woman Matt would have ogled before meeting Sandy. The question was, after the romance wore off, would he start ogling again, like our father had? Or would he abandon Sandy even sooner than my father had abandoned my mother?

My attention was suddenly drawn over Michelle's shoulder to where a small, plump figure waved her hand in the air. ''Excuse me, but my great-aunt is trying to get my attention.''

''I'll see you later,'' Michelle said, and as I walked toward my aunt, I saw her drift toward the small stage where the band was playing some sappy love song while Matt and Sandy danced. No doubt Michelle was gazing at her boyfriend, dreaming of the day the two of them got married. That's another thing a wedding did to perfectly sane people—it made them want to get married.

I had two great-aunts. Daisy was small and round and cheery. It was she who hailed me with an uncharacteristic worried frown creasing her brow. She was dressed in lilac lace, which almost clashed with her unusual shade of pink hair; rhinestones glittered on her ears and her ample bosom. One hand continued waving at me even though it was perfectly obvious I'd seen her and was coming. The other plump hand rested on the square shoulder of her seated sister, my Great-Aunt Prudence.

As different as silk from burlap, Daisy and Prudence nevertheless got along very well. My mother called them the "Family Eccentrics." When we were younger, Matt used to call them the "Looney Tune Sisters," to the amusement of no one but my father. I didn't want to think about my father, so I waved back at Daisy and made my way through the crowded reception to her table.

"Hello, you two," I said and leaned down to kiss Daisy's soft, wrinkled cheek and then the amazingly taut cheek of Prudence, who was sitting primly at the round table covered with tiny little roses and bowls of lacy bags of birdseed. With slate-gray hair and eyes, she was only a year older than her sister, but Prudence had refused to modify her looks because of age. She'd also refused to invest perfectly good money in a dress she'd wear only once, so she'd worn her severely cut, dark-blue shirtwaist.

If Great-Aunt Daisy looked as though she were ready

to meet the Queen of England, Great-Aunt Prudence looked as though she were waiting to catch a bus to Omaha. Wearing a saffron silk dress with a fitted waist and a full skirt and with my black hair pulled back and anchored with a bow, I hoped I looked as though I'd dressed for an occasion somewhere in between.

Prudence patted my hand. "Daisy's having a tizzy," she told me.

Daisy did indeed seem to be on the verge of mild hysteria. I scanned the crowd for my mother.

"Don't bother looking for *her*," Daisy said.

"Who?"

"Your mother," Prudence said, proving that both of them knew I was hoping to divert their problem—whatever it turned out to be—into my mother's capable hands.

Great-Aunt Prudence added, "She and Daisy got into a fight over Mr. Fu. She's told us we have to leave her house."

"She wouldn't!" I said as Daisy dabbed at her eyes with a linen hanky and sniffed a few times.

"She doesn't like my little darling," Daisy said. "Can you imagine?"

"He bit her mailman again," Prudence reported succinctly.

"I'm sure we can clear this up," I said, finally spying my mother playing mother of the groom with well-mannered ease. "Let me talk with her."

"Oh, would you please?" Daisy implored with watery eyes.

"Won't do any good," Prudence announced. "Your mother doesn't like animals, especially dogs."

"I'm sure there's just been a misunderstanding," I said, attempting to placate them.

As I turned to leave, Prudence caught my hand. "This must be very painful for you," she said. "I mean the wedding and . . . everything."

Daisy caught the drift of the conversation and momentarily put her own concerns aside to add, "Oh, yes, dear. It must bring back some dreadful memories of Johnny and—"

"There's Mother," I said, interrupting them because I knew if they kept this up, I'd tell them what I really thought about Johnny, and that would serve no purpose other than to further upset them. Gently disengaging my hand, I sidled past a few other guests on my way to intercept my mother.

By the time I got to her side, she was talking with a tall redhead and the best-looking man I'd ever laid eyes on. Like the woman, he, too, was tall but solid to her willowy. His face was rugged in a totally refined way, with sandy-colored hair touching the back of his collar. Two hazel eyes looked down at me. I felt my heart go THUMP; then it seemed to stop beating entirely until he smiled, which kind of kicked it back into gear.

Crazy. I returned his smile as I put my hand on my

mother's arm and waited for a lull in the conversation when I asked, "May I interrupt for a moment?"

She put her hand over mine. "Of course, darling. I want you to meet Amanda and Theo Brighton. This is my daughter, Matt's sister, Kylie."

Theo Brighton smiled at me again. He had lovely white teeth and a smile just crooked enough to transform it from nice to fascinating. He clasped my free hand and shook it slowly, warmly, charm oozing out of every pore. I was aghast to discover I was receptive to this charm even though it flowed from a married man.

The handshake seemed to last forty years, but in actuality was no doubt over in seconds, though Theo's fingers warmly pressed against mine as I slid my hand from his grasp. The woman said something I didn't catch, he told her she was right, and they excused themselves and walked away.

I stared at their retreating backs. I wouldn't have been able to pick the woman out of a crowd of one, but the man's face was, unfortunately, indelibly printed on my brain. As though he knew I was looking at him, he turned and our eyes met. Another smile was accompanied by something that looked like a wink!

"Did you want something?" Mother asked.

"Who is that man?" I whispered as Theo and what's-her-name disappeared behind a cluster of Sandy's relatives from Oregon.

"Just some old friend of your brother's; I really don't know him. What's wrong, Kylie?"

"Huh?" I looked back to her and swallowed. "Nothing."

"Isn't it a lovely wedding?" she asked.

"If you like weddings," I said briskly.

"Everyone likes weddings." Then she seemed to remember why I might dislike them, and she bit at her bottom lip. "I'm sorry. I know it's crazy, but I still have a hard time believing Johnny really did that to you."

"It's been two years," I reminded her.

"It doesn't matter how many years it is," she said softly.

My mother was forty-eight years old. She had the same dark hair that Matt and I had. She wore it so that it touched the top of her shoulders, with a sweep of bangs dancing above her eyebrows. Her eyes were brown and clear and intelligent, and people routinely took her for a woman a decade younger than she was. She ran her own arts-and-crafts store, painted and sewed and swam and competed in running marathons, and yet my father had left her for a younger woman. "Do you really like weddings, Mother?" I asked.

She smoothed her hands over the narrow skirt of her pink dress and said, "Of course I do. Look at Matt. He reminds me of your father at that age. In fact, all day I've been reminded of my own wedding."

"How can you even think about Dad?" I asked with a gasp.

She patted my arm. "The present doesn't completely obliterate the past, dear. Remember that."

"He's been gone ten years, and never once has he contacted any of us—"

"Like I said, it doesn't really matter how long it's been."

"And he left in the most stereotypical manner possible. He ran off with his secretary, for heaven's sake!"

"Your father always did have a penchant for clichés," she said. "Okay, we've both been burned by good-looking rascals. At least you found out sooner than I did. Now, Kylie, what did you want to talk to me about?"

Since it was fine with me if we dropped any mention of Johnny Page and any sentimental thoughts of my rotten father, I said, "Aunt Prudence and Aunt Daisy. I hear they've been given the boot."

"Don't be silly. I just told Daisy she'd have to put that miserable little beast of hers in a kennel. He bites people, Kylie."

"But, Mother, surely they won't be staying with you much longer."

She planted her hands on her hips and narrowed her eyes. "When they told me they were having their house painted inside and out and asked if they could stay with me for a few days, I said to myself, sure, why not? I have plenty of room, and I've always had a soft spot in my heart for the old dears. But that was three weeks ago, Kylie. Prue brought two cats, Daisy brought that . . . that . . . dog . . . and there hasn't been a peaceful moment since. Now, I'm willing to extend my hospitality, but not to that awful dog. I wouldn't mind the cats disappearing from the face of the earth too. The orange one sheds day and night, and the black one never stops eating, but I understand it's difficult to board those, so I'll go along—"

"Mother," I interrupted, "you know Aunt Daisy isn't going to put Mr. Fu in a kennel."

"Then they'll have to go home."

"But it's being painted."

"Then you take them."

"Me?"

"Sure. You live alone, you have an extra room—you take them."

"I hardly know them!"

"Then wouldn't it be a wonderful opportunity for you three to get closer?"

"You'd really cast them out on the street?"

"Not them, that mutt."

"Same thing."

"Then I really would."

I shook my head. "How you can get all mushy over a man who deserted you and yet be willing to abandon those two sweet little old innocent ladies to who knows what—"

"You don't understand—"

"I understand that you're not being very charitable."

"Maybe not," she admitted. "But if they insist the dog stays, then they're out."

"Okay, I'll take them in for a few days until the painters finish. It should be fun."

"Famous last words," she said, then kissed my cheek and floated off toward the buffet table.

I had no idea what had come over my usually kind mother. I went back to my great-aunts, asked them to come stay with me until the painting was finished, and was rewarded with two huge smiles.

Two years before, on my twenty-fourth birthday and in the midst of a personal crisis, I'd bought myself a house. I'd decided that I was going to make a life for myself, that I wasn't going to buy into the mentality that my life was on hold until some man made me complete. Johnny had left me, but I had the money I'd saved to begin our lives together, and I was determined to be happy, fulfilled, and independent all on my own, even if it killed me. Now I was the proud owner of two redwood trees, a scrappy patch of grass, three rosebushes, and a thirty-year mortgage.

The house still needed a lot of work, and the day after my brother's wedding, I awoke eager to get started painting the trim. My great-aunts were due to arrive that afternoon, so before opening the can of red paint, I mended the hole in the fence in the backyard so Mr.

Fu could frolic safely in the grass, and then I put clean sheets on the two twin beds in what I loftily called the guest room.

In some indefinable way I was looking forward to having my two great-aunts stay with me for a few days. Since marriage wasn't an option, I didn't plan on ever having children, and as I put a vase full of poppies on the table between the beds and opened the window to air the room, the thought crossed my mind that my maternal instincts must be kicking in. I immediately stopped fussing and went outside.

As I painted the trim from atop my ladder, I kept seeing Matt's face as he and Sandy left for their honeymoon. Big brother was definitely in love; I couldn't help but wonder if he worried that it wouldn't last, that he'd end up ten or twenty years down the line with a trail of broken hearts behind him, including his own.

I'd attended dozens and dozens of weddings over the last five years. Not only friends and family, but if a Barton's bride bought her wedding gown from us, and that of her bridesmaids, and if she registered with the store, then she got me on her wedding day to make sure her dress looked just right, to check on the groomsmen, to stay and help with the photographs. Hundreds of weddings.

Had I started out this sarcastic about marriage, or was it the fact that I now saw divorce announcements in the paper for some of my first clients? Or was it Johnny's fault? If I'd been ready to take the plunge myself, so to say, then at one time I must have been as wide-eyed and innocent as all the other young women I met in my job. This was hard for me to believe.

Could the whole thing possibly go back even further than Johnny? Could I still be recoiling from my father's abandonment? Sure, he'd left my mother, but I'd been sixteen at the time, and so in many ways it felt as though he'd left me too.

How old did a woman have to become to stop blaming her parents for her faults or at least her traits? I wondered and laughed at myself.

Then I thought of *him*, the man with the green eyes and the dark-blond hair, the man with the knock-'em-dead smile. I thought of that knowing wink he'd given me when he turned, the way his fingers had lingered when he shook my hand. The man was a flirt obviously, yet his wife was certainly a looker and seemed nice enough. Was it hormonal, this inability for a man to get next to a woman and not make a pass, covert or otherwise? And what was I doing, thinking about this guy? For every straying husband, there was a willing "other woman," and that was one role I wasn't about to fill.

The whole thing threatened to depress me, so I pushed all thoughts of weddings and men, especially *that* man, out of my mind and began painting.

I heard my great-aunts arrive before I saw them. At the time, however, I was cleaning paintbrushes under the hose and wasn't aware that the howling sound I heard was actually Mr. Fu protesting his cage. The noise got louder and louder until I finally looked up and saw a taxi pull up to the curb. The driver was out like a shot, and when his eyes met mine, I saw into the soul of a man near the end of his rope.

The noise continued as Daisy opened her door and struggled with Mr. Fu's cage. I hurried over to help her and was rewarded with a nipped finger as my hand strayed too close to the front bars.

"Ouch!" I said and almost dropped the cage.

"Be careful," Daisy scolded. "Mr. Fu is very delicate. Aren't you, sweetums?"

Sweetums growled.

The driver was helping to deliver, from the confines of the backseat, a larger carrier that held Prudence's two cats. He then dragged Prudence's and Daisy's suitcases out of his trunk, deposited them unceremoniously on the sidewalk, checked his meter, and announced, "That'll be ten bucks, ladies."

Prudence opened her purse and took out a bill. "I'm sure you are mistaken, young man," she said. "That's way too much."

He looked at the bill, which I could see was a five, and said, "Now, wait a second—"

I went into the house and took ten dollars out of my purse, figuring the man deserved a large tip. By the time I got back to the sidewalk, the cab driver and Great-Aunt Prudence were yelling— Well, the driver was yelling; Great-Aunt Prudence was just shaking her head—while Mr. Fu, still caged, barked.

I got between the driver and my great-aunt and pressed the money into his hand. "Just go," I told him. "Go."

He thanked me and left. Great-Aunt Prudence said, "You shouldn't have given in to him, Kylie. People will take advantage of you if you let them. You must be firm!"

Why did it occur to me that those words were going to haunt me until the housepainters finished my great-aunts' home?

Somehow we got everyone into the house. I'd never met the cats before. Coal Button was black and fat and shy, and the other cat, Mr. Phibbs by name, was a lanky orange-and-white-striped male who immediately made for my only good piece of furniture and proceeded to sharpen his claws. I shouted at him and out of the corner of my eye saw Great-Aunt Prudence's mouth draw into a straight line, so I said, "Will you make sure Mr. Phibbs understands he must go outside and scratch a tree?"

She nodded. "You never have to tell Mr. Phibbs anything twice," she assured me. "Nor do you need to raise your voice."

"Good," I said.

Just then Daisy released Mr. Fu, who immediately ran over to me and snarled. He was smaller than the orange cat, a high-wire bundle of stringy gray fur and beady black eyes, with sharp little white teeth he liked to bare when he growled, which he seemed to like to do with alarming frequency. Daisy introduced us, and when I tried patting his head, he nipped at my hand. Daisy laughed and announced that he must like me, that he hadn't been nearly so friendly with my mother.

I decided right then that I owed my mother an apology.

As my great-aunts unpacked their bags, I tried to make friends with Coal Button, but he/she was extremely timid and would only come close enough to sniff my fingers. I was crouched down, trying to coax him/her out from under the sofa, when I felt a stinging bite on my heel. I looked around to find Mr. Fu attached to the bare skin of my heel with his sharp teeth.

Jumping to my feet, I screamed in anger and pain, but the dog just renewed his efforts. I picked up my foot (dangling the dog) and jerked it twice, which finally disconnected him and sent him scooting across the carpet. He landed by the chair with a woof and a renewed attack.

"No!" I cried as I scrambled up on the coffee table.

"What was that?" Daisy called from her room.

I looked over to find Prudence in the bedroom doorway, staring at me with wide eyes. She stepped aside as Daisy rushed toward her mutt. Gathering the little beast into her plump arms, she cast a surly glance at me and demanded to know what had happened.

"The little brute bit me," I said with an attempt at

a placating smile. I got down off the coffee table, feeling like a fool, like a full-grown woman climbing on top of a piece of furniture to escape a mouse, which, come to think of it, Mr. Fu did rather resemble.

"Nonsense!" Daisy insisted.

"She kicked him," Prudence said.

"I didn't really kick him—"

"Yes, you did—I saw you. Not that I blame you."

Daisy glowered at both of us as she carried her dog into the room. Crooning comforting words in his floppy little ear, she closed the door.

"Thanks a lot," I told Prudence as I hobbled into the kitchen to clean the blood off my foot.

"No bother," she said. "Anytime."

Chapter Two

*T*he next morning I discovered it was a relief to leave the house and drive to work, because by the time I struggled, bleary-eyed, to the kitchen, both relatives were up and running. Prudence had all my wash done and was hanging it out on the line, and Daisy had cooked me a huge breakfast. In the interest of starting things out on a positive note, I'd eaten pancakes and sausage under the baleful gaze of a snarling Mr. Fu without mentioning that I preferred just coffee with maybe the occasional slice of toast. That night I would sit them down and establish some ground rules, I decided.

Barton's was the biggest store in our small town. Within its formidable walls customers could find the goods to furnish their homes, stock their linen closets, set their tables, cook their dinners, dress the whole family, get a perm, buy a television, and, most im-

portant, plan their entire wedding—clotheswise—
along with the help of yours truly, me.

As I hurried to my desk, Madge Wilkerson looked
up from her cash register and said, ''Good morning,
Kylie.''

Due to the big breakfast, I was a few minutes late.
I nodded at Madge and dumped my purse into my file
drawer.

Madge wandered over to my department. ''Mrs. Sullivan was looking for you,'' she said.

Mrs. Sullivan was our supervisor. I nodded to show
that I'd understood the message, but Madge wasn't
finished yet. ''I told her you aren't often this late.''

''Five minutes,'' I said incredulously. ''I'm a whole
five minutes late.''

''And your first appointment called and canceled a
few minutes ago. I took the call for you.''

I knew why she'd taken that call when she system-
atically ignored most others; with Mrs. Sullivan standing by, what else was she supposed to do? Taking calls,
even if it wasn't your department, was part of what
she and I were being paid to do. I flipped through my
appointment book and said, ''The call was from Sue
Garvey?''

''That's right. Seems she and her intended had a
little bit of a spat over the weekend. She told me she
never wanted to see the rat again.''

Brides sometimes canceled appointments, but eventually most of them made up with their fiancés and

rescheduled. I always tried very hard not to get too involved in their problems, because if they changed their minds, I didn't want them to worry that they'd said too much to me and be embarrassed to contact me again. I hoped Madge had been diplomatic.

She was in her mid-fifties, with curly gray hair and wire-rim glasses that tended to rest near the tip of her nose. I knew she'd been married for thirty-some-odd years; she wholeheartedly believed that a marriage was best started with a gala wedding, pull out all the stops. I'd never admitted how I really felt about the whole thing, that if the couples spent the same time and energy on their marriage as they did on the wedding day, things might work out better. But I think she knew how I felt, and I think it bothered her that someone like me had the job she felt in her heart she could do better. Maybe she was right.

I got down to work, which meant first contacting Mrs. Sullivan, who said she hadn't been looking for me in particular; she'd just been looking around the store. When I apologized for being late, she said, "Yes, Madge told me you were late. I'm sure it won't happen often."

"No, of course not," I said and went back to work. My first priority was checking on the whereabouts of a designer silk bridal gown. I'd had to order it months ahead, but the dress was stunning, even by my rather jaded tastes. Made of French lace, the beaded bodice was see-through, and the full long skirt was enhanced with more beads, some of them in the color and shape of pastel flowers. These same flowers covered the bodice, giving it the modesty it required to be worn in public. I'd never seen the dress except in a magazine that Carla Milton, the bride, had brought to my attention. We'd struggled to get it ordered through one of our vendors.

The dress had set Carla (or perhaps her father) back several thousand dollars. It was now two weeks overdue, and Carla was getting a little antsy. As we'd been on a strict time schedule, I didn't blame her. I got on the phone and tracked it as far as Portland, Oregon; I was promised that the dress was on its way south to Cypress Bay, California, and that Barton's would have it by the middle of the week. I told them that if it didn't show up, I was going to set upon them Carla's father, lumber baron Harry Milton, and they'd be sorry. I then spent a few minutes ordering veils from our vendor, looking up only when I sensed a woman standing next to my desk.

It was the redhead from the day before, the one with the husband I couldn't get out of my mind. I'd remembered her as pretty; now I saw that in actuality she was beautiful.

"Didn't we meet yesterday at Matt's wedding?" she asked.

"Yes, but I'm sorry, I've forgotten your name," I said, standing.

"Amanda Brighton. I thought I recognized you. Isn't this a coincidence?"

I agreed it was, and then, as if materializing out of one of my daydreams, Theo appeared behind her.

Amanda turned to him. "There you are, Theo. Do you remember—" She paused and, looking back at me, said, "Now it's me who's forgotten your name."

"I never forget a name, especially when it's attached to a face like yours," Theo said, dazzling me with another one of his killer smiles. "Kylie, right?"

"Yes, Kylie Armstrong," I said, but along with feeling thunderstruck, I felt annoyed. How dare he flirt with me!

"Theo has an eye for beauty," Amanda observed dryly.

"I admit it," he said, looking right into my eyes. "After all, I may have grown up here, but I've been away for several years, so in essence I'm new in town. Maybe you and I could have dinner sometime—"

Amanda laughed. "You're a fast worker," she told him.

What was this, I thought, some kind of new-age marriage that didn't even try to adhere to the rules of fidelity and respect and—

"My brother is a flirt, Kylie, but not an idle one, are you, Theo?"

"No, not idle," he agreed as he pulled a chair out for Amanda. Then her words finally sank in: He was her brother!

"Then you're not . . . married?" I stammered as I sat down.

As he sat opposite me, he said, "Not me!"

"Theo is married to his work. He doesn't have time for a wife, do you, Theo?"

"Well, I won't when I get settled, that's true. Right now I have time for dinner—"

"Stop right there, big brother. Romance Kylie on your own time. We're here today for me." She turned to me and added, "Mike finally asked me to marry him." She wiggled a diamond-encrusted engagement ring in front of my face. "I don't want to wait around until he has time to change his mind."

Theo chuckled. "Poor sucker."

"Be quiet," she told him, then added in my direction, "Don't ask me why, but I dragged Theo along to help me choose a dress."

"You dragged me along because after poor old Mike popped the question, he headed for the hills."

"He's out of town on business until this evening," Amanda told me, sparing a quick frown for her brother. "Besides, I hate to admit it, but Theo has excellent taste. Do you have the time to show me your wedding gowns, Kylie?"

"As it turns out, I do." I said it to her, but my gaze strayed to her brother. It did so all on its own, because I was determined not to act on my obvious feelings of attraction to this man. He was the kind of man it was dangerous for me to be around, the kind who put foolish ideas into my nice, practical brain.

Amanda cleared her throat and reminded us once again that they were there for her.

Theo sat back in the chair as Amanda and I worked our way through the gowns I had in stock. As they were samples, most of them were a size ten or twelve, so they'd fit the average figure. Amanda was a lot smaller than that, but when Theo pointed out a silk and lace dress with a plunging back adorned with a wide bow, she wanted to try it on along with a few others. In the end, it was the one he'd chosen that made her gasp when she saw her reflection in the huge mirrors.

"How long will it take to get it in my size?" she asked as she admired herself. We'd moved into the large dressing room, and she stood on a circular stage with mirrors all around her. I took a veil with a silk shantung braided headband off the veil rack on the side wall and set it atop her smooth red hair; she looked like a model for a bridal magazine.

"It takes about four months," I told her.

She counted on her fingers. "If Mike and I get married around Christmas, that's six months from now."

"The dress will be here in plenty of time," I said.

"I want to show it to Theo. Shall I go out there?"

"I'll bring him in here," I told her. "You're pinned together under that veil, you know."

So I went back to my desk and told Theo his sister

wanted to see him. I was intensely aware of him as he followed me into the dressing room. He leaned his long body on the doorframe and whistled. Amanda giggled, and even though the compliments that poured from his chiseled lips were meant for her, my heart did that THUMP thing again.

"The front is kind of plain," she said.

"The front has your face to light it up. Besides, everyone looks at the back, not the front. Isn't that right, Kylie?"

"It *is* the part people see the most," I agreed.

"An expert's opinion," Theo said, smiling at me until my legs felt like two cooked noodles.

By the time I'd ordered her dress and veil and the proper petticoats and made an appointment to meet with Amanda's matron of honor to choose a dress for her ("Kylie, I'm having only one attendant. I want a small wedding but a traditional one.") it was time for my next appointment.

Theo lingered by my desk as Amanda walked away. He leaned down and said, "Will you have dinner with me tonight?" but before I could answer him, he swore under his breath and added, "I forgot about the banquet I have to attend. How about tomorrow night?"

"I don't really date much," I told him truthfully. It had long ago occurred to me that if I didn't want to fall into this joined-at-the-hip trap, there was no reason to go about tempting fate by being alone with attractive males. Especially attractive males like the one currently staring into my eyes, the kind who called out to something primitive in me, something hidden and deep that didn't give a darn about what I thought.

"My next bride has just arrived for her appointment," I pointed out.

He followed my gaze to a young woman with that customary bridal glow about her. She was standing next to Madge, who was making a big production of not looking my way.

"We won't call it a date," he said. "We'll call it dinner. You do eat?"

"I do eat, but usually, like I said, I eat alone."

"It sounds kind of lonely."

"Not at all."

"Then you're a woman with a life plan, and it doesn't include me."

"Nothing personal. It doesn't include anyone. I'm fine all by myself."

"Obviously. Still, that older woman over there seems to be keeping track of you. Is she your boss?"

"Wouldn't she love that! No, she just wants my job."

"And she might get it if I plant myself on this desk and refuse to leave, right?"

I laughed. "We wouldn't call it a date?"

"Nope."

"I don't know a thing about you."

"What's to know? I'm not a life partner, remember, just a dinner partner."

"You're a pest."

"I'm waiting."

"Oh, all right. But just dinner."

"Right. By the way, I'm a veterinarian," he said. "I'm going into practice with Dr. Stewart. Know him?"

I shook my head. Madge's looks were becoming both more frequent and more interested. I suspected the woman had long ago discovered just where to stand so that she could hear every word I uttered. Paranoid? Who, me?

"Kylie?"

"What time shall we meet?"

He stood up straight and tall and gorgeous. "Are you in the phone book? Yes? Then I'll pick you up at seven. I'm looking forward to it."

I smiled and told myself I wasn't.

When I returned home, I saw that Mr. Phibbs had plastered himself to the inside of the front window; his eyes were closed against the glare of the sun. "Tough life," I mumbled to myself as I wondered how Daisy and Prudence had gotten along on their first day in my house.

I was greeted at the door by the smell of roasting chicken and the sound of barking. It was a high-pitched sound, the kind that made the fillings in your teeth hurt.

"Hurry, hurry, dear," Great-Aunt Daisy said as she bustled from the kitchen.

At first I thought she was talking to Mr. Fu, who seemed intent on keeping me from entering the house. I stepped over the mutt quickly and fixed him with a stern stare, which he ignored. When it became evident Daisy was speaking to me, I asked why.

"Because Prue and I were talking this morning. You're getting on in years, Kylie; you'd better get with the effort and catch a nice young man before you lose your feminine wiles."

"My what?"

"You know, dear, your allure."

"I don't want to catch a nice young man," I snarled as I plopped myself into my good chair. The shy black cat scooted under the couch.

"Now, now, you can't go mourning Johnny Page forever."

"I assure you that I am not mourning Johnny Page!" I insisted.

She shook her head. "Kylie, you don't want to end up an old maid."

"But you and Prudence never married," I said.

"Tut, tut. What's that got to do with anything? Hurry now."

"Aunt Daisy, why exactly do you want me to hurry?" I asked without making a move to get up.

"Because we've invited our grocer and his son for dinner. Mr. Oliveras is such a nice man. Prue says he has the best prices in town, and she should know— she checks all the ads. She found chicken wings on sale there this morning, and I made Jell-O— Can't you hurry, Kylie?"

"You invited them here tonight?"

"Well, of course. This is our home, isn't it?"

That left me speechless. Obviously I should have had that talk about ground rules with them before I left for work that morning.

"Hurry, dear, they'll be here any minute. Go put on something pretty."

Along with a certain feeling of unreality was an equally strong feeling that I could argue all night and it wouldn't do a bit of good. Meanwhile a couple of strangers would show up, and the ensuing scene would shame me down to my socks. So, feeling like a spider ordered to bait her web, I plodded into the bedroom and changed clothes.

I was just brushing my hair back from my face when Daisy knocked on the bedroom door. "Is Mr. Fu in there with you?" she called.

"You can look, but I find it highly unlikely," I said.

She came into the room, and while she looked under bed and dresser, I went into the bathroom and brushed my teeth. When I returned to my room, I found her sitting on the edge of the bed, wringing her hands.

"You haven't found him yet?"

"No, dear, and I'm worried."

"He was inside when I came into the house. Maybe Aunt Prudence put him in the backyard—"

"Oh, no, dear, she wouldn't do that. Mr. Fu never goes out alone; Prue knows that."

"I see. Well, I'll help you look some more, but I wouldn't worry. I bet he's asleep in the back of a closet or something."

She stood resolutely. "I imagine you're right. Well, I won't let that little rascal ruin your chances for happiness, Kylie, so come along, dear—let me look at you."

She adjusted my blouse and fluffed my hair, and when she was sure I couldn't be improved upon without a lot more work than we had the time for, she led the way to the kitchen.

I set the table and tried not to let one little brain cell think about the coming evening, when I would be thrust together with the grocer's son by two old ladies who had never been married but who thought I should be. I didn't have the heart to do what I wanted to do, which was scream that I did not let anyone make social plans for me without my knowledge and stomp out of the house, but I did grind my teeth a lot.

Daisy was still skittering around the small house, looking for her dog, when the doorbell rang. "Get that, dear, will you?" she sang as she pushed the couch back against the wall.

I opened the door to find two medium-sized men

with identical smiles. I invited them inside, and by the way both Mr. Oliveras and his son looked me up and down, I had no doubt that the intention of my great-aunts' invitation was very clear to all concerned. I believe I groaned.

Bob Oliveras, the son, was about thirty. I'd once heard that CIA and FBI men were supposed to be good looking without being noticeable—the idea was to blend into the background, be easily forgotten, be neither too tall nor too short, too thin nor too fat, too blond nor too dark, too. . . . Well, that's what I thought of when I looked at Bob, an impression helped along by the light-gray suit and the pale-blue tie. He wasn't too anything.

We ate chicken wings so disguised in some sort of cream sauce that it was hard to tell what they were, drank a glass of white wine from the bottle Mr. Oliveras brought, nibbled on cherry Jell-O and Cool Whip for dessert. With the strange food and with strangers seated around the table, I felt like a guest in my own home. It occurred to me that my great-aunts had been in residence for little more than twenty-four hours. By the time their house was painted and they left, I imagined my life would resemble a grain field after the locusts depart.

"How long have you lived with your great-aunts?" Bob wanted to know. We were seated together on the left side of the table.

I said, "Not long."

"Now, Kylie," Prudence said firmly. She looked at Bob and added, "Kylie is such a tease. Good sense of humor is important in a wi . . . in a woman, don't you think, Bob? No, this is Kylie's house; Daisy and I are the guests. She works at a good job, makes good money. She has her own car. . . . Is it paid off yet, dear?"

Sure I was blushing the color of a tomato with a sunburn, I yearned to stammer something like, "Shall we show him my teeth?" but was saved by the phone. I was off my chair and into the living room by the second time it rang.

"This is your neighbor, Ida Fontaine, from down on the corner," a woman said.

"Yes, Mrs. Fontaine, what can I do for you?"

"It's what I can do for you. I was out walking earlier today, and I saw two older women out in your front yard. They had a rather . . . noisy . . . little dog with them."

I explained who everyone was.

"Well, that same little dog is outside my house right now barking up a storm at the neighbor's cat, which it chased into one of my trees. I tried to do something about it but, frankly, the dog scares me. I think you'd better get it before someone shoots it."

"Of course," I told her. "I'll be right there."

After I hung up the receiver, I ducked into the dining room—a nook off the kitchen—and told everyone what was up. Daisy was ready to leap out the front door, but Prudence caught her arm. "Let Bob and Kylie go, dear."

They exchanged meaningful glances, and I believe I groaned again. Not waiting for anyone, I stomped out of the house. Bob was right behind me.

"They're insufferable," I said as I followed the barking we could hear coming from the corner.

"They're sweet," he said.

I wondered how he felt about house guests.

Mr. Fu was under a small maple tree. From high in the branches, when the dog stopped to catch his breath, we could hear a cat growling and spitting. I tried to pick up the little dog, but he reached around and snapped at my hands. One tooth grazed a finger, and I yelped in pain.

Ida came out onto her porch. "Nasty little bugger, isn't he?" she said. "Could you use an old towel?"

"We don't need a towel," Bob told her. He approached Mr. Fu, who snarled and snapped at him too. Bob looked at me and then back at the dog. This time he attempted a surprise attack, which left him on his knees, clasping thin air.

"Bob?" I asked as I wrapped a Kleenex I'd found in my skirt pocket around my bleeding digit.

Ignoring me, Bob got to his feet, took off his jacket, and put it across the porch railing. He called Mr. Fu by name, made clucking noises, and stepped slowly up to the snarling miniature monster. Bob did a fancy little two-step, but Mr. Fu danced nimbly to the left.

I think I began to like this nondescript man about the time he rolled up his sleeves and tried staring Mr. Fu down. This time when he approached, he lunged, and it would have worked if Mr. Fu just weren't so darn fast. As it was, Bob ended up face-down on the grass. Sensing victory, Mr. Fu pranced up to Bob's face. The man escaped a "nosectomy" by mere seconds as he leaped to his feet and regained the porch. Mr. Fu happily resumed yapping at the cat in the tree.

I'm afraid I was laughing by this time. As Bob brushed off his pants, I said, "If I were you, I wouldn't go on risking my life trying to capture that animal bare-handed."

He grabbed his jacket and chuckled. "Since you're giggling like a schoolgirl, I guess I'm not doing much of a job impressing you with my cunning and agility. Okay, let's eat crow and take the towel."

Ida had already retrieved the towel. She handed it to me, and I threw it over the little bundle of snappy fur. While Mr. Fu fought the towel, I swooped him into my arms. The vocal remonstrations continued, but the mean end was temporarily decommissioned, so I was able to lug the dog back down the block. He struggled and growled and yipped, but I was bigger and stronger, and he was stuck.

We were across the street from my house, waiting for a car to pass, when Great-Aunt Daisy could stand it no longer. From her position on my porch she cried, "Mr. Fu, darling! My baby!"

At the sound of her voice, the small dog renewed his efforts to escape. He wiggled out of the towel and hit the ground running. As I watched in helpless horror, Mr. Fu dashed straight into the path of the approaching car.

There was a squeal of brakes, a scream from Daisy, a gasp from Bob, but I watched silently, as though it were a film, a piece of fake reality. The moment of surrealistic numbness didn't last long.

The car pulled up to the curb. Daisy ran out to the street and kneeled over her prone dog; Prudence stood on the porch with her hands over her mouth, Mr. Oliveras at her side. Bob took my elbow and steered me out to the middle of the street.

I cried out when I saw the dog's side heave. He was alive! We used Ida's towel to put over his small body and lift him into Daisy's arms. It was hard not to reflect that it was the first time anyone but Daisy had lifted him without coming to some kind of harm; it was also the first time he'd been quiet since he arrived.

I heard Bob reassure the motorist, a sobbing teenage girl, that it wasn't her fault. He asked me if I wanted help, and when I told him that we could handle everything, he and Mr. Oliveras left. Prudence put Mr. Fu's still body into his carrier and loaded it into the front seat of my car as Daisy called her vet, got the answering service, and scribbled the address on a piece of paper as she cried out what had happened.

Scooting me out to the car, she said, ''No, Kylie,

I can't come with you. I can't bear to see Mr. Fu in pain. Just call me right away, as soon as you know something.''

"I'll stay with Daisy," Prudence said.

I drove as fast as I dared. For hours I'd wished the little dog would be zapped by a meteorite or stung by a swarm of yellow jackets, yet now as he lay still, his breathing shallow, all I wanted him to do was survive.

It was Dr. Stewart's clinic, but it was Theo Brighton who met me at the door. He was even more shocked to see me than I was to see him; after all, I'd known there was a fifty-fifty chance he'd show up at Dr. Stewart's office, while he'd had no idea after talking with his answering service that I'd be the one delivering the wounded pet.

He was dressed in a black suit and a blue shirt. A flowered tie brought out both colors. There was no getting around it—he looked elegant. "We got you away from something," I observed.

"A banquet in honor of Mike's work with disadvantaged kids," he said. "I took a cab over here as soon as I heard from the service."

He took the carrier from me, and we walked down the hall into one of the examination rooms. He took off his jacket and shrugged on a white smock; then he washed his hands. As he carefully took the small dog out of the carrier, I noticed how well-formed his hands were, not overly big but strong and as handsome as the rest of him.

"The animal was struck by a car?"

"That's right. His name is Mr. Fu—"

"I looked through his file while I waited for you to get here," he interrupted softly. "I called Mort, but his wife said he's in bed with a fever and the chills, so it looks as though I'll be covering for him tonight."

"Who is Mort?"

"I'm sorry. I forgot you brought Mr. Fu in for a relative."

"My Great-Aunt Daisy."

"I see. Well, Mort Stewart is the veterinarian here. I'm his new partner."

Deftly, he examined the small dog whose sides, I was relieved to note, were still moving up and down although his breathing still seemed shallow. Theo listened to Mr. Fu's chest with a stethoscope, pulled back his eyelids and looked into his eyes, examined his gums, took his pulse. Then he looked at me and said, "This little fellow is in shock. His pulse is accelerated, his mucus membranes are pale, there's a certain amount of congestion in his chest, and his pupils are dilated. What we need to do is to stabilize him."

"How do you do that?" I asked.

"First I'll do a scout lateral X ray of the chest, abdomen, and the pelvis; then I'll set up an IV catheter with two milligrams of Azium on a slow drip and put him on a heating pad to keep him warm. I see he has a small abrasion or two, so I'll clean those off and cover my bases with a little penicillin."

"So he'll be okay?"

Our eyes met. "Well, a lot depends on what we find when we X-ray him. I'll be truthful—I'm worried, but I'd rather get the results of the X ray before I speculate anymore."

I bit at my lip and said, "What do I tell Aunt Daisy?"

He stared at me a moment. "When an animal goes into shock, everything rushes to the center, you know, to protect the brain and the vital organs. What we need to do is replace the fluids, keep him warm, and get some antibiotics and the dexamethasone—that's the Azium—into him. If the X rays show no internal injuries to the liver or the spleen or whatever, then he will recover. If he makes it through the night—"

"You mean he might not make it?" I asked, appalled.

"I'm afraid that's a possibility."

I nodded. It was going to be a very long night. "If you took a cab here, how are you going to get home?" I asked him.

"I guess I'll call another cab," he told me as he put antiseptic on a sterile pad and gently sponged the cuts on Mr. Fu's side. When he was finished, he looked up at me and said, "Let me fix your finger for you."

I'd forgotten about the dog bite on my finger. Theo swabbed it gently with antiseptic and wrapped a bandage around it. I said, "I'll wait for you and give you a ride home. If you want."

He looked up, and his beautiful eyes looked right

into mine. "I may be some time getting this little guy stabilized."

"I know."

"Well, it certainly couldn't be misconstrued as a date, could it?"

"I believe we'll be perfectly safe," I agreed.

He smiled. "Thank you. I accept."

"Okay. Take your time; do whatever you have to do. I imagine there are a few fascinating magazines in your waiting room that will amuse me."

"Not unless you fancy magazines about cats and dogs."

"I'll live. Just let me use your phone."

I called Great-Aunt Daisy and imparted the news with guarded enthusiasm. She reacted with silence. I heard Prudence asking her what I said, and then suddenly Daisy broke into heart-rending cries. The phone clattered as though the receiver had been dropped. A moment later Prudence demanded, "Kylie? Kylie? Tell me what you told Daisy. She's having a tizzy."

So I repeated my report. As I was finishing, Theo ducked his head into the office I was using and said, "The X rays don't look so good, Kylie. I won't need a ride home, after all."

I put my hand over the receiver and said, "You aren't going to spend the night here?"

"I don't dare leave him." He disappeared down the short hall toward the back of the clinic, and I uncovered the receiver.

"Who was that speaking?" Prudence demanded.

"The doctor."

"I've heard Mort Stewart's voice a million times, and it doesn't sound like that!" Her voice was a firm whisper, as though she didn't want her sister to hear what she was saying. "Where are you, Kylie?"

"At Dr. Stewart's office. Dr. Theo Brighton is Dr. Stewart's new partner."

"And it's this Brighton fellow who is looking at Daisy's dog?"

"That's right."

"Oh, dear. Daisy won't like that. What did he say?"

"He said he's going to stay with Mr. Fu all night, so, you see, the dog is going to have his own personal physician."

"Hm—" Prudence said.

When she hung up the phone, a feeling of foreboding settled in my heart. I went back to say good-bye to Theo. Mr. Fu lay on a small heating pad, an IV running into him. His breathing had accelerated into shallow panting.

Theo ushered me outside and said, "I'll do my best."

"I know you will."

"Good night, Kylie."

"Good night, Theo."

"Until dinner tomorrow, that is."

"Yes," I said and, despite the desperate situation that lay between now and then, smiled at him.

* * *

Daisy insisted on sitting by the phone just in case Dr. Stewart should call with news. I sat up as well because I knew it wouldn't be Dr. Stewart calling but Theo. I kept waiting for Prudence to tell her sister the true identity of Mr. Fu's attending veterinarian, and when she didn't, I decided to tell her myself. A stern look and a flagrant change of topic convinced me that Prudence thought it better not to say anything. As she knew Daisy better than I did, I kept my mouth shut.

The call came after only an hour. I'd nodded off with the shy black cat in my lap. The ringing jolted the cat awake; he/she jumped off of my lap and darted under the couch as I leaped to my feet. I got to the receiver right before Daisy.

"It's Theo," he said. He sounded tired and discouraged.

"How is Mr. Fu?"

A long pause prepared me for bad news. "I'm very sorry," he said. "Please tell your aunt that I tried everything, but the little guy was just too severely injured. His internal organs— Well, really, I should be giving her this report."

"I don't think that's wise right now."

"Okay. Please tell her he never regained consciousness and I don't believe he suffered. Will you tell her for me?"

"Yes," I managed to squeak. "Thank you."

"I wish there were better news. Tomorrow she needs

to contact the office about the disposal of Mr. Fu's body. We can arrange it for her if she wishes."

"I imagine she'll want to take care of that herself."

"I understand. Again, I wish I could have done something for the dog."

"I know. Good night, Doctor."

I turned as I recradled the receiver, unsure of exactly what to say, but Daisy knew without being told. She burst into tears.

Chapter Three

*P*rudence and I had done everything we could think of to comfort Daisy, but she was too distraught to listen to our words of condolence or drink hot tea or even to sleep. The next morning, when I finally tore myself away from my great-aunts, they were seated on the sofa, the fat black cat peering out between their ankles from his/her hideaway, the orange one draped across Daisy's lap as though consoling her.

I was late again. When Madge said "Good morning" while glancing at her watch, I'm afraid I just cast her a surly look and went straight to my desk. I hadn't slept much, I was heartsick for Daisy and for Theo too, and I had an appointment in fifteen minutes with the Nightmare Bride; I didn't need Madge keeping track of me.

A Barton's buyer bought our wedding gowns from thirteen different vendors, veils from six. At any given time there were forty or more long dresses hanging on the wall behind my desk from which prospective brides could choose. My appointment that morning, a woman of about thirty who confided that this was her third wedding, didn't like anything we had to offer. She'd been in four times to look at our dresses, and even though I'd offered to order this one in ivory and that one in beige or this one with a lace train and that one street length, she still found nothing to like about anything. That's why I'd privately dubbed her the Nightmare Bride.

Her real name was Fiona Catalina. Many was the time I'd speculated on that name. It sounded like it belonged to a showgirl or an exotic dancer, and her looks supported this conclusion.

"This dress reminds me of dress number one," she said, referring, I assumed, to her first wedding dress. "I was twenty years old then, and I liked fluffy things. Now this dress, this dress is even uglier than dress number two. I was twenty-five then, and I thought I should look like a princess. I'm thirty now, sophisticated, worldly. Dress number three must reflect that."

A wedding every five years! My head reeled.

She was a statuesque woman with a cap of bleached-blond hair and the reddest lipstick I'd ever seen. She wore a royal-blue dress and dangling silver earrings with little balls and chains that moved when she talked. In my emotionally and physically exhausted state, the earrings mesmerized me.

"Are you listening to me?" she asked.

I blinked my eyes and forced my gaze from the earrings. "Of course. Nothing is right."

"And you're the only store in town. I guess I'll have to drive to San Francisco."

I saw a light at the end of the wedding-dress tunnel. I said, "That's an option," aware as the words left my lips that Madge had placed herself within hearing distance. Oh, well.

"But I really don't want to," she said, pouting her berry-red lips.

I gathered up the last ounce of energy I had and asked, "Have you thought about wearing a long formal dress instead of a bridal gown?"

"What do you mean?" she asked, her attention suddenly snapping back to me.

"Come with me." And, once more tearing my gaze from her silver earrings, I led the way to a rack of sequin-studded gowns. I chose an emerald-green number with glints of gold running through it. The dress was form-fitting, exotic, flashy. I said, "As it's your third wedding, I don't see why you can't wear whatever you like. I'm sure this dress would complement your figure." Consulting the tag, I added, "It also comes in royal/silver, black/gold, jade/gold, red/gold, and pink/silver."

"Pink?" she asked, visibly perking up.

"Yes, pink."

"Have you seen it in pink? Is it dark pink or light pink?"

Mentally crossing my fingers that she favored the shade the dress came in, I said, "It's a light pink."

She clapped her hands together. "Wonderful. You're a genius. I'll try this one on."

And she did, and she liked it, and we ordered it, and she gave me the twenty-five percent deposit, and I watched her leave the store and hoped she'd never come back except to pay for the rest of the dress when it arrived. That reminded me of another dress that hadn't arrived—namely, Carla Milton's dress. I called her house, got her mother, and told the woman the dress was promised by the next day. The good lady reminded me the wedding was less than two weeks away and that it really would be nice if Carla was wearing that dress, and I agreed that yes, it would.

After that call I made an in-house call up to alterations, where I warned Sheila that we would be having a priority fitting within the next couple of days. I hoped.

After lunch I got a call from Sue Garvey. She somewhat shyly admitted that she and her intended had made up, and she was wondering if I could work her into my schedule. If it wasn't too much bother. If I could find the time. If she hadn't blown her chances forever by canceling. I mentally cursed Madge for whatever she'd said that made Sue feel this way, leafed through the appointment book, asked her about Friday afternoon, and she said, fine.

It was almost time to call it a day when a woman approached my desk. She was smiling widely, as though she knew me, and though she did look familiar, I couldn't place her.

"Kylie, so this is your little lair," she said loudly. "Gee, I don't know what you don't like about this—it's wonderful in here. Look at all these gorgeous dresses!" she added as she fingered the soft poly-satin of a wedding gown.

Her name popped into my head the moment she touched the dress. It was Michelle Green from Matt's wedding, the girlfriend of the guy in the band, the woman I'd been so indiscreet in front of. As I nervously glanced over my shoulder to see if Madge was close, I said, "Michelle, how nice to see you again!" Madge, thankfully, was nowhere in sight and so had presumably not heard Michelle's comments.

She sat down opposite me. "You'll never believe what happened after your brother's wedding."

I looked down at the ring finger of her left hand. A modest but sparkly solitaire diamond confirmed my suspicions. "Congratulations," I told her. "You're the second woman to become engaged after that wedding. I wonder if there was something in the punch."

She laughed. "But I have a problem," she said, though her eyes were twinkling and her pretty mouth was turned up at the corners. "My fiancé is leaving on a tour in three weeks, and he wants me to go with him—as his wife! Isn't that marvelous?"

"It's the nicest problem I've encountered today," I said.

"It's all so spur of the moment, but I do want a wonderful dress. I don't suppose there's time to order one?"

"No, but there are several on the rack, and we have an excellent alterations department. Shall we see what we can find?"

She took her time looking, but I could tell that the traditional long white gown didn't hold much appeal for her. One after another, she barely glanced at long flowing dresses of lace and satin and pearls.

Every once in a while Barton's buyers purchased a dress I was sure would never leave the store; we had one in stock now. Somehow it didn't surprise me when Michelle stopped at that exact dress.

It was a very short—mid-thigh—sleeveless white satin flapper dress with four-inch handmade roses around the hem. Michelle took the dress off the rack and inspected every detail. She whistled when she saw the price tag, but I had a feeling it wouldn't deter her; she'd fallen in love.

She put the dress on. Her blond hair hung in gentle waves to just above her shoulders, and her body was good enough to carry the whole thing off. "I could wear this afterward," she said.

I agreed.

"What do you honestly think?"

"I honestly think you do the dress justice," I said.

"I could wear white high heels and long white gloves. And I want a veil. One like that."

I handed her a long, transparent veil affixed to combs. We tried it on, and she beamed. "I might not look like the figure on top of a wedding cake," she said, which I thought was a definite understatement, "but I will be noticed."

I laughed. "You have a sense of the dramatic."

"That's true—I'm a Leo. Okay, I'll take it," she said.

Sheila from alterations came down and suggested taking the dress up a little at the shoulders. I told Michelle that we couldn't begin alterations until the dress was fully paid for, and she said no problem. I saw why when she whipped out her trusty Barton's charge card.

As we decided on a delivery date, Michelle said, "This has all happened so fast, I can hardly believe it."

"It's nice to see you so happy," I told her. I had my doubts that that happiness would last long, but that was just because I was a card-carrying cynic when it came to marriage. I don't know if Michelle was tuned in to my thoughts or if she just remembered our conversation at Matt's wedding, for all of a sudden, in her loud voice, she asked, "Did you really mean what you said, that you hate weddings?"

Naturally, *naturally*, Madge was now standing close by. Was it my imagination, or had the woman begun hovering? What did it matter? She'd heard Michelle; there was no way she could not have heard Michelle. I said, "I told you that that was just a joke."

She laughed. "Well, I feel like I ought to invite you to our wedding. It's going to be very small, but if you really hate them as much as you said you did that day, then I don't want to impose on you—"

"I'd be delighted to come," I insisted, hoping she'd take the hint and stop burying me in my own hole.

"Really? Okay, but I warn you, there will be champagne and miniature rosebuds and rice and all that."

"Splendid!" I said.

Michelle frowned, but at least she shut her mouth. From the corner of my eye, I saw Madge smile, speculation running like an electric current through her eyes as they peered over the top of her glasses.

I stopped off at my mother's arts-and-crafts store on the way home because she'd left a message with the office while I was at lunch asking me to. She was just letting her last customer of the day out the door when I arrived. She was wearing a tight pair of jeans and a pink sweatshirt with little flowers painted all over it. I knew she'd done it herself when she taught a class in fabric painting.

"Thanks for coming, darling," she said as she turned the Open sign to read Closed. "Want a cup of stale coffee or a can of Coke or anything?"

"Nothing, thanks." As I followed her toward the

back of the store, I marveled at all the stuff she'd crammed into such a small space. There were racks and shelves and displays of everything imaginable, from Styrofoam balls to straw wreaths to bottles and jars and cans of paint, to dozens of spools of ribbons. There were two long tables that she used for her classes, and stacks of magazines and books for ideas and help.

Mother started ringing out the cash register, and I said, "I suppose you want to talk about Mr. Fu and Aunt Daisy."

"I told you he'd drive you crazy, Kylie. Don't say that I didn't warn you. How she can put up with him—"

"Wait a second, Mom. You don't know?"

"Know what?"

I told her about what had happened to Mr. Fu, and we both spent a moment speculating about how the little dog had gotten outside. "Maybe he darted out when I came through the front door," I said. "If so, then it's my fault."

She frowned as she closed the register drawer. "I didn't particularly like the little beast— Oh, all right, I'll be honest, I detested him. But poor Daisy, she just adored him. Don't you go blaming yourself. It sounds to me as though everything would have been fine if she hadn't called for him while you were still across the street."

"I hope she never thinks of that," I said. I glanced up at the wall clock and saw that it was six o'clock and realized with a jolt that I'd completely forgotten about my coming dinner with Theo Brighton. This encouraged me as it meant that I wasn't harboring any hidden agenda about romance and the like.

It suddenly occurred to me that my mother had been talking about something and I wasn't sure what it was. I caught my father's name and then something about dating other men, but I couldn't put it all together. "Could you start over again?" I interrupted.

"You do look a million miles away. What were you thinking about?"

"I'm sorry. It's just that I'm having dinner with the veterinarian who was with Mr. Fu when he died, and I realized I'd forgotten about it."

"Mort Stewart!"

"No, the new vet. You met him at Matt's wedding. His name is Theo Brighton. He was with the redhead."

"Oh, I remember. He's quite good looking, isn't he?"

"Yes," I said.

"Then you go home and get ready. You don't date nearly enough—"

"This isn't a date. You know how I feel about men and marriage—"

"Spare me the lecture, Kylie," my mother said with a grin.

I grinned back. "I guess I am a broken record."

She put her hand atop mine and said something that wiped the grin right off my face. "Have you ever stopped to consider that you might still be in love with Johnny Page?''

For a moment I was too stunned to speak.

Undaunted, she continued. ''He left you so abruptly, dear, without a word, without a good-bye except for that ridiculous note. Haven't you ever wondered if your feeling of animosity toward getting involved with an-other man is really your way of staying available in case Johnny ever comes to his senses and returns to Cypress Bay? I hear he never married his sister-in-law. In fact, I hear she's back with her husband—''

This was more than I could bear. ''Mother, please.''

For a long moment I could feel her gaze burning into me, but I didn't trust myself to meet her eyes. She withdrew her hand. Determined to change the subject and put from my mind forever the ridiculous idea she'd brought up, I said, ''Why did you want me to stop by?''

She bit at her lip, a habit I'd recently noticed that I'd acquired too. Was biting a lip a genetic thing? Was attracting a good-looking man who ran out on you a genetic thing as well?

My mother said, ''You have a date, Kylie. We'll talk later.''

''Not a date—''

''That's right, I forgot. But you go on. I've changed my mind; I don't want to talk about . . . this . . . yet.''

''What does that mean?''

"It means I've changed my mind. A woman is allowed."

I stared into her eyes and saw that she really had changed her mind, that she really didn't want to discuss whatever it was she'd called me about. I knew she'd come around in her own good time and that pressuring her would be counterproductive, so I said, "Okay. By the way, have you heard from the blissful honeymooners?"

"What do you think?" she asked with a wistful smile, and I had that sinking feeling she was thinking of Dad again.

"I think that they flew to Hawaii and forgot all about us."

"So do I," she said. "So do I."

I arrived home to find Daisy still moribund over Mr. Fu's death, but I had expected that. The little dog had been so nasty and antisocial that she'd been his only supporter. At the same time she'd been the one human the animal tolerated, so naturally she'd think he was pretty special. I wished there were something I could do to help, but Prudence said just to leave her alone, that in time she'd feel better.

Of course, my mother's ridiculous suggestion still rang in my ears, so it took me a moment to figure out what they were talking about when they started in about the funeral service.

"At the Shady Pine Pet Cemetery," Daisy informed

me. "Mr. Fu is to be interred tomorrow afternoon at three o'clock. You will be there, won't you?"

I thought of my work record that week and knew there was no way I could ask Mrs. Sullivan to give me half of the afternoon off so I could attend a dog's funeral. I said, "I can't. I'm sorry, but I can't get off work. How will you get there if I'm not here to drive you? Can it possibly wait until the weekend when I can help—"

"Nonsense. We'll take a cab," Prudence said.

Daisy sighed. "I understand how much you'd like to pay your respects, Kylie, but I also understand the ways of the world, and I know it's not easy to take time off from work. Mr. Fu would understand too, I'm sure of it."

"I'm . . . er . . . glad," I stammered. The one thought that kept running through my mind was that I wouldn't have to be around when some hapless cab driver tried to collect his fee from Prudence.

Prudence also said, "That nice Bob Oliveras called, Kylie. He wanted to know how Mr. Fu was, and he was quite distraught when he heard the bad news."

I thought of the one and only time Bob Oliveras had had any contact with Mr. Fu and decided Bob probably wasn't quite as "distraught" as Prudence thought.

As though passing along a real earth-shaking piece of news, she folded her hands together, leaned toward me, and added, "He asked about you. I think he likes you, Kylie."

"He's a very nice man," I said casually. "Well, I have a dinner appointment tonight, so I'd better go take a quick shower and get ready. Will you two be okay alone?"

"Did you say you have a date?" Daisy asked, perking up a little. "With Bob?"

Until two days before, my great-aunts' contact with me had been minimal. We weren't exactly part of one another's lives; I didn't know their friends, they didn't know mine, and yet upon moving in a short forty-eight hours earlier, they'd decided that I couldn't find a man of my own and that the only male I knew who would qualify as a potential mate was one they found. It irritated me, but I knew explaining how I felt about the issue of dating would be wasted breath on them. Just a few more days and they'd go home and things would return to normal. I said, "No."

"Then who is he?" Prudence asked.

"A friend."

"Does your mother know him?" Daisy asked.

"Well, she's met him—"

"But does she know his family? Young people are so careless about things like that nowadays. The Oliveras family has been in Cypress Bay for four generations. Our father used to shop at Mr. Oliveras's grandfather's store when it was still on Fig Street. Didn't he, Prue?"

"You would be hard put to find a more respectable family," Prudence said. "And I happen to know Bob wants to settle down. He works at the store, you know. Someday he'll be the owner. A woman could do a lot worse.''

I laughed through clenched teeth and felt my good intentions take a hike. ''I am twenty-six years old,'' I said stiffly. ''As you pointed out to Bob Oliveras last night, I'm self-supporting. What you may not understand is that I have no intention of marrying anyone . . . not Bob, not anyone, not ever, so I really do think it would be better if you didn't pry into my affairs, don't you?''

Gasping, Daisy said, ''You're having an affair!''

''No, that's not what I meant. I meant that I have friends of my own.''

''You put it rather rudely,'' Prudence said as she stroked the orange cat.

She was right; I had. ''I'm sorry,'' I apologized, realizing the reason I was reluctant to come clean with them about Theo was that I knew Prudence would remember his name, and I wasn't sure if she'd told Daisy yet about the true identity of the vet who had cared for Mr. Fu. Of course Theo wasn't responsible for what had happened, but I wasn't sure Daisy would understand that, and the last thing I wanted to do was subject Theo to a scene of any kind.

I tried smiling again, apologizing, even offering to fix them both dinner, but Daisy said (rather tartly) that as I had places to go and strangers to see, she would fix their dinner herself. She pranced into the kitchen, her dignity like a shield, her steps reminiscent of her recently departed dog. It was the first sign of spunk I'd seen in her, so even though I sighed deeply and went to my room like an errant child, I was relieved that she'd shown a spark of her old spirit.

By the time seven o'clock rolled around, I was perched on the bench by the door. At the first sign of Theo's car, I fully planned on sprinting out the door.

"Now, Kylie," Prudence said reproachfully, "you go on back to your room, and we'll call you when your young man arrives. It doesn't look good to be so desperate. When you hear me call you, just say that you'll be right out and wait five minutes. Daisy and I will find out a little more about him—"

"You didn't listen to a word I said, did you?" I interrupted.

"You're just tired. We all are after the night we had." She looked over her bony shoulder toward the kitchen and added, her voice in a conspiratorial whisper, "I didn't tell Daisy about that new doctor attending Mr. Fu. Now, if we can just keep her from asking Dr. Stewart about it, we'll be okay."

We were staring at each other as coconspirators do when I heard a car pull up in front. I quickly kissed Prudence on her cheek, called out a hearty good night to Daisy, and escaped my own house.

If Theo was surprised to be greeted on the sidewalk, he didn't show it. He smiled at me, but he looked tired, as though he'd had the same troublesome night I'd had.

While his smile was still of the killer variety, it now had an edge of frailty to it that made him seem very vulnerable and very desirable. Warning flags went up in my head.

"You look beautiful," he said.

"So do you," I told him truthfully. He was wearing another dark suit, this one charcoal gray. He had on a paisley tie in shades of blue and rose, and his sandy hair was combed back from his face. He was almost too good to be true.

"Is one of those two old ladies peering out of your front window your Great-Aunt Daisy?" he asked as he opened the car door for me.

I didn't need to look back to answer. "The plump one with the pink hair. She and Great-Aunt Prudence are staying with me while their house is being painted." It occurred to me that it might behoove me to check into the progress of that project the next day.

"I would like to go inside the house and explain what happened to her dog," he said as he slid in behind the wheel. "The only reason I don't is that from the way you bolted out the front door as I pulled up, I get the feeling you'd rather I not see her."

"Not yet," I admitted. "Daisy was very . . . attached to that dog."

"Of course she was," he said matter-of-factly. He started the engine, waved at my great-aunts, and we were off.

Almost immediately he asked, "Why?"

"Why?"

"Why don't you want me to speak with her about Mr. Fu?"

This was not the way I wanted to start the evening, but I couldn't think of a single thing to say except the truth. "She thinks it was Dr. Stewart who worked to save Mr. Fu. Prudence thinks it would upset her terribly to know it was someone else."

He nodded thoughtfully. "Sooner or later she'll discover the truth."

"Why do you say that?"

"Because the truth always has a way of emerging. Haven't you noticed?"

"You may be right," I admitted. "But meanwhile, at least she'll have time to recover from her loss."

"You know best," he said, an insane comment if ever I heard one. I let it pass and was glad when the subject died.

He was a good driver, and I was so exhausted that I just settled back in the seat and closed my eyes. I've found there's something very liberating about speeding along in a car at night, something romantic and yet comforting. Maybe it makes me feel like a child again, when my parents drove and Matt and I sat in opposite corners of the backseat and dozed. Everything was safe then; my parents were in control. All I had to do was be a child, and they'd take care of the hard stuff.

I opened my eyes not only because that thought had proved to be an illusion, but because the car was slow-ing down. I hadn't thought to ask where we were going; truth of the matter, I didn't really care. Just being in the car with Theo was enough. More flags.

He'd pulled into the parking lot of the Huckleberry Inn, the fanciest place in town. I was glad I'd put on my prettiest black dress and highest heels.

Dinner was served in a semicircular booth. Theo sat very close to me, but somehow it didn't feel crowded. There was a fake fire burning in the fireplace right by our table which provided flickering light but no heat, something we didn't need in June. I ordered scallops, and he did too, along with a bottle of white wine; music from the piano bar drifted in from the lounge next door.

"This sure seems like a date, doesn't it?" I asked as we split a piece of lemon cheesecake.

He took a sip of coffee. "Not to me. It does to you?"

"No," I amended quickly. "Not really. No, of course not."

"Relax," he said, smiling.

When the check came, I insisted we split it fifty-fifty, and though he grumbled and complained, I was relieved when he finally agreed.

After dinner we walked down Main Street. It was deserted, but with Theo's shoulder close to mine, I found myself alarmingly content.

"It's hard, losing an animal," he said as we walked.

"You're still thinking about Mr. Fu. Was this the first time an animal died while in your care?"

"Not by a long shot. You're not a veterinarian very long before an animal dies or the owners have one put to sleep. It's part of the business, the bad along with the good. But it never gets easy, and you always feel awful for the animal's master."

"But at least you have a job you love," I said.

He stopped and looked down at me. As coastal weather can do, even in the summer, ours had changed during the time we were in the restaurant. The clear skies had clouded over, and a fine mist now coated everything. We were standing outside a florist shop, and the lights from within hit Theo's face. Tiny drops of mist sparkled in his hair.

"How do you know I love my job?" he asked.

It took me a moment to answer because he was so close, it was darn near intoxicating. I said, "I can hear it in your voice."

"And you don't love your job?"

"How do you know that?"

"I didn't. I inferred it from your statement. But why wouldn't you like your job? You bring so much happiness to so many people."

"Happiness," I mused. "Is that what you think marriage is?"

"Don't you?"

"Maybe the wedding ceremony, but that's just the icing on a very large, very big cake."

"So you don't believe in marriage."

With him standing that close, I had to remind myself of my convictions before answering, "No. Do you?"

"Not for me," he said. "But Matt sure looked happy, and Amanda is floating on a cloud."

I nodded. "Maybe it will work for them, but the current statistics say that only a little over one out of every two marriages makes it."

"So your brother or my sister will someday go through a divorce—is that what you're suggesting?"

"Yes. I don't know how people have the heart to fall in love," I said.

"Then why are you and I here, Kylie?"

"What do you mean?"

"If we honestly don't believe in love and marriage and family, then why are we drawn to each other? Why did we have such a hard time concentrating on Amanda yesterday? Why are our hands touching?"

I reclaimed my traitorous hand. "Chemistry," I whispered. "It has to be tempered with common sense." And common sense would protect me, I assured myself, from making another mistake like Johnny Page.

"I see. Well, the mist is getting serious. I guess we'd better be getting back."

"I think that would be wise," I told him.

During the night my imagination filled in the blanks my mother's inquiry had created. Johnny came back to Cypress Bay, just as vital and handsome as ever.

He strode right into my house and picked me up like I was a favorite throw pillow he'd gone off and forgotten. I awoke trembling with the heat of his kiss on my lips—the heat of a remembered kiss I'd tried so hard to forget. It took a long time, lying awake in the dark, to regain sleep, and when I did, it was full of dreams, though Johnny was mercifully absent.

Before I left for work the next morning, I scouted the backyard, looking for a place in the fence where Mr. Fu could have escaped. I found it. The little rascal had dug under the new patch—he was small enough that it didn't take much space for him to gain freedom.

I hadn't let Mr. Fu into the backyard, and Daisy certainly hadn't, which meant that Prudence had. As far as I knew, she hadn't mentioned it to Daisy, but she must be overwhelmed with guilt, and as I walked back into the kitchen, I wondered what I could do to help her.

The smell of eggs and muffins greeted my nostrils. Daisy was putting my breakfast on the table as I poured a cup of coffee; of course, I hadn't the heart to tell her I didn't want to eat in the morning, not when it seemed to give her so much pleasure to feed me.

"How was your date last night?" she asked as she sat down opposite me.

"It wasn't a date," I said. "These muffins are delicious. Aren't you having any?"

She sighed. "I don't have much of an appetite, dear. I wouldn't cook at all if it wasn't for you."

"But what about Aunt Prudence?"

"Oh, mercy, Prue doesn't eat breakfast. She just sips juice, that's all."

"Then you mustn't cook just for me," I said, sensing my way out of this morning ritual.

"Oh, I don't mind, dear. It makes me feel useful. Well, he certainly was a good-looking boy."

"Who?"

"Your date. Prue and I saw him through the window. 'Course, Prue says men who are too handsome are bound to be trouble."

"He wasn't my date."

"Of course he was. He called for you, didn't he? He bought you dinner? He was your date."

"I bought my own dinner."

Her mouth fell open. "He didn't look like *that* kind of young man," she said primly. "Well, never you mind, darling. Bob Oliveras called again last night. It's good you weren't home. It's good he thinks you were out with the competition. Prue says there is no better way to intrigue a man than by playing hard to get."

It seemed pointless to argue with her, as neither she nor Prudence listened to a word I said. I just took a bite of egg and tried to look bored.

"Anyway, Bob invited you to attend the community theater tonight as his guest. It's the benefit performance of *The Sound of Music*. I hear it's very good. You're to be ready by seven-thirty."

It took me a moment to swallow the bite in my mouth without choking. Finally I gasped, ''You didn't accept for me?''

''Well, you weren't here. I hate to remind you of this, dear, but you're not getting any younger. You can't go on hating men forever just because you found one rotten apple.''

''I don't hate men,'' I said, knowing full well that this wasn't the point. I took a deep breath and added, ''Aunt Daisy, I know you're just doing what you feel is right for me, but you mustn't try to throw me and Bob Oliveras together. I'll be very frank with you. I don't date. Period.''

Her face lit up with a smile. ''Then this is perfect because he also invited Prue and me. We're very excited.''

''Wait a second—he invited all of us?''

''That's right. One can hardly call it a date when there is one gentleman and three ladies, can one? This ought to be right up your alley.'' She stood, thereby punctuating her comments, and I, wishy-washy as usual, knew I was going to the community theater that night.

Trying very hard not to sound eager, I said, ''How is your house coming? Are the painters almost finished?''

''I leave all of that to Prue, Kylie, though I believe she told me yesterday that things are progressing nicely. I'm not sure exactly what she said because yesterday I was so distraught about my poor baby . . . my poor little darling dog.''

I swallowed and said, ''I'm so sorry, Aunt Daisy. I know how terribly fond you were of him.''

''He was my little friend.''

''I know, darling.'' I patted her hand. ''I'm sorry that I won't be able to attend his burial.''

She nodded. ''I know. But it's okay; don't worry about it. I shall try to be stoic for Prue's sake.''

''Why must you be stoic for Prudence's sake?''

Daisy leaned close. ''Hasn't it occurred to you that she must have let my little darling out the door in the first place? Think how she must feel. Prue puts on a hard-boiled act, but I know she was almost as fond of the little dear as I was.'' A pair of tears formed in Daisy's eyes. She blinked them away and said, ''Finish your toast, dear. We don't want you to be late for work.''

I wasn't late to work. In fact, I beat Madge Wilkerson. To make things even better, the Milton wedding dress had arrived, and I was able to call Carla and ask her to come in that afternoon for a fitting. She sounded almost weak with relief. The only thing that marred that first hour of work was a call from the Nightmare Bride. She'd decided pale pink wasn't so good, after all, and asked me to cancel the order. Since I hadn't called it in yet, that was easily done, but when she assured me that she'd be down later that day to find another dress, I wanted to scream.

During the morning I helped a fifty-year-old woman find a dress for her upcoming marriage to a local doctor. She chose a street-length formal dress of pale-yellow silk lace with a scalloped hem and tiny seed pearls sewn all along the bodice.

On the opposite end of the spectrum, a pudgy, pale teenager wandered in. She had very little money and a wedding planned for two weeks hence. I steered her away from the more expensive gowns to a rack of sale dresses. Miracle of miracles, we found one that fit her pretty well, one of the samples that were now out of stock so that the price had been reduced from eight hundred dollars to under two hundred.

Even with that drastic cut, I could see the girl couldn't really afford it, but she counted out the proper bills from a wad she dug from her jeans pocket and laid them on the desk, and I wrote out a receipt. I told myself that maybe a beautiful wedding would form a foundation for a stable marriage for the girl, who looked and acted as though she were fifteen, but I couldn't help feeling that the two hundred dollars might be better spent on rent or food.

One thing was certain: It wasn't any of my business, but had Barton's merchandise been mine to dispose of as I wished, I would have thrown in a veil, petticoats, long white gloves, and shoes, all for free.

During my lunch break I got in the car and drove

over to my aunts' two-story Victorian house. It was heavy with gingerbread; newly painted pink with white trim, I thought it looked like a structural rendition of a wedding cake.

I went inside the open front door. All the furniture had been piled under sheets in the middle of every room. The sitting room looked finished, but everywhere else there were signs of work in progress. I went out the back to find part of the painting crew eating lunch.

"Hi," I said. The two men looked totally unsurprised that a stranger had just entered the backyard via the house, a reaction (or lack thereof) that somewhat alarmed me.

The older man nodded. He was wearing painting overalls and a Giants baseball cap. A sandwich made neat trips to his mouth.

I told them who I was, which didn't seem to impress them much; then I said, "How long do you figure you'll be finishing up in there?"

The younger man looked up from his container of pasta salad and shrugged. "Boss says it should take us another week, maybe two. The old ladies don't seem to mind how long it takes, so part of the crew started another job last week."

This earned the young man a pointed stare from the older man. The young man went back to his salad, and I said, "So how many of you are working on my great-aunts' house?"

"You're looking at us, lady," the older man said. "Don't get in a huff, though. They're not paying us enough to bust a gut over anything."

I nodded feebly and wondered if they'd let me help them on weekends, because if they didn't get going, I had the awful feeling my life was never going to return to normal.

Chapter Four

*C*arla Milton stood on the podium looking like another model for a bridal magazine. I'd noticed wedding dresses had that effect on women; there was just something about them that made even homely people look good, and as Carla was quite stunning already, the dress just improved things—if your taste ran to dewy-eyed women in love who were willing to put all their trust and their future happiness in the hands of another human being.

The model image was slightly tarnished by the fact that Carla was shaking like a leaf. An average-size woman with glossy dark-brown hair, she'd once been calm and controlled and very amusing, but now she seemed nervous and edgy. I hoped that nothing was wrong between her and her fiancé.

The dress was as beautiful as the magazine picture had made it look; as this isn't always the case, I was profoundly relieved. Carla's jittery hands seemed to be in constant motion, straightening nonexistent wrinkles on her skirt or darting to her head to adjust the wide-brimmed hat adorned with beaded flowers that she'd chosen to wear instead of a veil.

Sheila, the alterations woman, studied the hem, walked around Carla, and looked at the fit of the waist and shoulders, the length of the long, pointed sleeves, the drape of the skirt. At last she said, "These are the shoes you're going to wear with the dress?"

Carla looked down at her silk pumps and said, "Yes. What's wrong? Is something wrong? Are the heels too low, or is the color wrong—"

"They're fine," Sheila said calmly. "I just need to know so I can hem the dress properly. And what about the petticoats?"

"Everything is as it will be," I said.

As Sheila pinned the hem, Carla smiled nervously at me. "Are you sure this dress looks okay?" she asked for the third time.

"It looks wonderful, doesn't it, Sheila?" I asked.

"Beautiful," she agreed.

"And, Kylie, you'll be at the wedding?" Carla asked anxiously.

"Next Saturday evening, nine o'clock," I said.

"At the Silvercloud Country Club. It's an outside nighttime wedding, so remember to bring your mosquito repellant if it's warm or your sweater if it's not."

I laughed. "A bride with a sense of humor is a rare and beautiful thing. I'm glad to see you've kept yours."

"It's that or go nuts," she told me as Sheila and I helped her take off the dress. "My mother has really gone bonkers. She spent three hours the other day trying to decide if we'd made a mistake by not having Jordan almonds in the candy cups along with those little pale mints. Then she decided that tiki lamps weren't good enough and ordered hurricane lamps, and I don't even know the difference. I'm not even sure there is a difference. Believe me, Kylie, you'll understand the craziness if you ever get married."

For a second I was plunged back into my own bleak little past. The church had been lovely. It had been early spring, and my mother and I had decorated it with lilacs and tulips. My dress was very simple, just yards and yards of satin with beaded, embroidered organza appliques with pearls and sequins trailing down the back. I was off in a small changing room at the back of the church, the church was filling with people, organ music was playing, voices filtered through the closed door. . . .

The decisions had all been made. The caterers were setting out food at the reception hall, the band was fine-tuning its instruments, the photographer was ready for my grand entrance, piles of presents littered my mother's spare bedroom. The only thing missing was my father, but since he'd been missing my whole adult life, I was handling it all right. Besides, Matt was standing by to walk me down the aisle. I was ready.

And then Johnny's best man had come into the room, carrying a small sealed envelope. His face should have warned me, but I was too nervous and too excited to see. I tore open the note, expecting some last-minute vow of love and enduring faithfulness and instead received the shock of my life. In a nutshell, Johnny said he couldn't go through with our marriage, that he'd fallen in love with his brother's wife and they were running away to Mexico and he knew I'd understand.

Later, after everything had been dealt with by my poor mother and brother, after I'd retreated to my mother's house to cry myself into oblivion, it was the word "know" that got to me. Not "I *hope* you'll understand someday," but "I *know* you'll understand." He was very, very wrong. I hadn't understood.

Was my mother possibly right? Had I wrapped myself in a cocoon of indifference not because I'd decided to forgo marriage and all the commitments I felt sure a man couldn't honor, but because the memory of Johnny was still so strong in my heart that I harbored romantic delusions that he and I could possibly get back together?

It had been good once; there was no denying that. A woman doesn't fall in love for the first time in her life with a man, promise to be his for eternity, rearrange her future to include him without giving it a great deal of thought. I'd been so sure of Johnny. . . .

"Kylie?" Carla asked, bringing me back to the present with a painful jerk. "Are you okay? You look kind of pale."

Sheila and the wedding dress were gone, and Carla was buttoning the last button on her blouse. I said, "It's nothing. Let's arrange a delivery date, shall we?"

Too busy with her own thoughts to worry about mine, Carla tied her shoelaces and sighed deeply. But before she left the dressing room, she said, "You will remember to come, won't you, Kylie?"

"To your wedding? Of course I will. Silvercloud Country Club, nine o'clock, but I'll be there at least an hour early, toting sweater and/or mosquito repellant."

"And you'll stay for the reception?"

"There's no need—"

"Yes, there is!" she screeched. She lowered her voice, but her eyes held a degree of panic. "I told you things are about to drive me nuts, but what I didn't tell you is this premonition I have."

"Premonition?"

"That something awful is going to happen at the wedding or afterward . . . I don't know, I just have a feeling."

"Called wedding-day jitters," I consoled her. "You're just having yours a few days early."

"It's more than that," she insisted. "Please say

you'll stay for the ceremony and the reception too. Everyone in the world is going to be there; I'm sure you'll find people you know. Kylie, you will stay, won't you?''

''Of course,'' I assured her, but the thought of another wedding reception did little to lift my spirits.

At that exact second the Nightmare Bride strode up to my desk, and I knew my day was going to deteriorate from the sublime to the ridiculous.

''Blue fades me out,'' Fiona Catalina said.

''Okay. No blue.'' I'd seen her wear blue any number of times, and I didn't think it faded her out at all; on the contrary, I couldn't imagine anything that would fade this woman.

''Do you have anything in gold lace?'' she asked. ''I saw a picture in a magazine once.''

''No. But you know what? You have plenty of time, and we're due for a shipment of new formal dresses a week from Monday. Why don't I issue you a refund for the deposit on the last dress and you come back in then?''

''Do you think there will be anything in gold lace?''

''You never know.''

She agreed to my plan. I knew I was only putting off the inevitable, but at the time it seemed like a very good idea.

*   *   *

Perhaps I lacked a sense of civic pride, but halfway through *The Sound of Music,* I wondered why anyone would subject themselves to untrained voices and borderline acting when they could rent the movie at the video store and listen to Julie Andrews do the whole thing properly. As six local children sang "Do Re Mi" a beat behind the orchestra and half a note flat, I hazarded a glance at my great-aunts, who were seated to my right. Their eyes were glued to the stage, their expressions rapturous. I looked to my left and found Bob Oliveras watching and listening just as intently.

I was one of the first people out of the junior college auditorium (the site of all of Cypress Bay's finer cultural events) for the intermission. Bob was right behind me, but my great-aunts were slow to begin with and even slower when they met one of their old neighbors. I left them talking to the woman, hoping that seeing her might remind them how much they missed their house, which would thus prompt them to hurry the painters.

We stood for a moment as the crowd pressed around us. Bob finally said, "I was sorry to hear about your Great-Aunt Daisy's little dog."

"They buried him today at the pet cemetery. He was a little monster, but she loved him."

"I notice you're wearing a bandage on your finger where he bit you that night."

I looked down at my hand. "It doesn't seem so bad now that the poor little fellow is gone, does it?"

"I remember the whole event with a certain amount of fondness," he said. "It was the only time I got to spend alone with you that night."

Our eyes met, but my gaze drifted away at once. Uneasy with the implied meaning of his words, I wasn't sure what to say. Bob filled in the gap by asking if I wanted a glass of complimentary champagne.

"Complimentary?"

"This is a benefit performance. Dad buys a few tickets every year, and this year I got to use them."

"It was nice of you to ask us along," I said. "I don't much care for champagne, but punch would be nice."

"Coming up. I just want you to know that I didn't ask *all* of you along," he added before he departed.

"You didn't?"

He turned back to me. "No, I called to ask just you, but somehow Prudence made it sound like you didn't go out with a man without an escort, and the next thing I knew, you were a package deal."

"Still think they're sweet?"

"Ah, they're just trying to do what's best for you. Well, I shall return." As he fought his way through the crowd, I looked around for my two sweet little old great-aunts and saw Theo Brighton instead. Any hope that he might not see me fizzled out as he waved and made his way over to where I stood. Had I really hoped he wouldn't see me or come to speak with me? Who was I kidding? Of course I hadn't. I was turning into a mess of contradictions, and it was all his fault.

"Well, well," he said, staring down into my eyes. I noted that all the usual things that happened to me when I saw him were happening again—i.e., weak knees, thumping heart, heightened senses. Something new happened too, something that caught me off guard. I felt myself smiling at the sight of him, pleased just to see his face and hear his voice, just to be standing in the same room with him.

I made myself look away from his face. "How do you like hometown theater?" I asked.

"It's . . . charming."

"Really?"

"Do you want an honest answer?"

"Yes."

He lowered his voice and leaned so close, his breath was warm against my cheek. "I don't think much of it. The actress playing Maria is twenty years too old for the part, and those kids make the sound of fingernails being drawn across a blackboard sound lyrical."

After I laughed, I asked, "What are you doing here?"

"Mort and his wife dragged me along. What's your excuse?"

"I came with my great-aunts and a . . . friend."

"I noticed a pause, so I presume the friend is a male," he said. He'd buried his hands in his pockets and stood staring down at me with a devastating grin on his well-shaped lips.

"Well, he is, actually. He's their friend, really."

"Oh. An older gentleman, then?"

"Well—"

"Because we all know how you feel about dating."

"Yes—"

"And I suppose you insisted on buying your ticket?"

"Actually—"

"Because if he bought it, who knows what demands he might make later? He might want to hold your hand or even kiss you."

"You really are a fiend, aren't you?" I asked, laughing.

"Let's just say that if this man treated you to this evening, then I demand fair treatment."

"What does that mean?"

"It means I demand a date. And don't say it—I know, you don't date. Then I demand the same sort of evening this man is getting."

"I could not sit through this performance another time," I said.

"Neither could I. Something comparable, then."

"You can phrase it any way you want, because the man is just the son of a friend of my great-aunts and—"

At this moment Bob emerged from the crowd, car-

rying two glasses of champagne. He handed me mine
and smiled expectantly at Theo.

"I decided tonight deserved champagne," Bob announced, waiting for an introduction I was loath to
make. For one thing, I didn't like champagne, and I'd
told him I'd prefer punch, so I was peeved that he'd
ignored me. For another, I didn't trust Theo not to say
something I'd find embarrassing.

I don't know what drove him to do it, whether it
was some kind of reaction to finding me talking with
a very good-looking man, or maybe he'd been sipping
the wine as he fought the crowds—at any rate it was
Bob who did the outrageous thing, not Theo. Bob put
his arm around my shoulders.

There was nothing I could do about it except shrug
it off or yell, "Bob, really!" both of which would
have made the situation even more awkward than it
already was, so I did nothing. As I introduced the
two men, I saw that Theo's eyes were brimming with
curiosity, while his mouth battled with another grin.
I was relieved when I saw my great-aunts approaching.

Bob's arm fell immediately upon their arrival. I was
so preoccupied wondering what that silly gesture of
Bob's had meant that the bigger problem, Daisy and
Prudence coming face-to-face with Theo, didn't enter
my mind until two more people joined us.

"This is Mort Stewart and his wife, Bonnie," Theo
said, introducing me to his partner. Mort and Bonnie

appeared to be in their late fifties. They both looked hearty and healthy, as though they rode horses or climbed mountains.

After Dr. Stewart shook my hand and cast a speculative glance at his young partner, he patted Daisy's arm and said, "And how are you doing? I know it is very hard to lose a pet. I'm delighted you're getting out with your friends."

"I'm doing better," she said, suddenly choking up.

I saw Prudence look at me with alarm, and I found myself biting my lower lip, but we were both as helpless to stop what was going to happen next as we'd been to save Mr. Fu.

"We had such a nice graveside ceremony today, Doctor, and I want you to know, I realize you did everything you could to save his life."

He patted her arm again. "I'm convinced that there is absolutely nothing I could have done for the poor little fellow that Theo didn't do. He's a bright fellow, Theo, a darned good veterinarian. Cypress Bay is lucky he agreed to come back here and go into practice with me."

Theo looked properly abashed. I finally found the courage to look at Daisy. She was staring at Mort Stewart with wide eyes under her fringe of pink bangs, and then her gaze moved along to Theo.

"*You* were with my little dog?" she asked.

Theo nodded. "As I told Kylie, the little guy didn't

suffer. He never came out of shock, but his body was just too traumatized—''

"He didn't even know you!" she blurted out.

Prudence took Daisy's hand and squeezed it. "The house lights are dimming, dear—"

"You killed Mr. Fu!" Daisy said. She didn't yell it, but her voice was loud enough to turn the few heads still left in the reception area and raise a few eyebrows too.

"Ma'am—" Theo implored but was cut off.

"And you lied to me," she said, turning her attention to me.

Mort Stewart took Daisy's arm. "Now, Daisy—"

"Don't you touch me!" she spat, tearing herself from his kindly grasp. "I trusted you." Furious, she turned to Bob and asked, "May I trouble you for a ride home, young man?"

Bob looked at me, and I nodded. Looking absolutely bewildered, he said, "Of course."

"I'll go with you," Prudence said, and I watched miserably as the three of them made for the door.

Mort patted Theo's arm this time—apparently the man was a great patter—and said, "Don't let it get to you, Theo. Daisy has always been a little too attached to that dog of hers. She didn't mean what she said. She'll forgive both of us once her common sense returns."

As Mort and his wife went back into the auditorium,

I wondered if he really believed what he'd said; I knew she'd meant every word.

"Well," Theo said, "I didn't expect an escape from this place would come with such a high price tag, namely peace of mind, but it's almost worth it."

I looked from Mort Stewart's back to Theo's face. "Are you leaving?"

"Yep."

"But what about the Stewarts—"

"We came in separate cars. Mort will figure it all out; trust me. I happen to know you need a ride."

I nodded, set the untouched glass of champagne on a folding table, and together we left the auditorium and made our way along the street. Theo stopped in front of his car and said, "It seems a shame to stop walking, doesn't it? Such a beautiful night."

"So many stars," I whispered.

"I suppose you're anxious to get home and defuse your great-aunts."

"Not particularly. I love them both very much, but, frankly, they're driving me nuts. Maybe this will get them steamed up enough to move back into their partially painted house or at least get them to spur the painters on. I just feel awful that it included you and Dr. Stewart."

"We've both faced worse things, believe me."

I thought of the scene that awaited me at home and wasn't sure *I* had.

Theo reached in front of me and unlocked the passenger door. Then he looked down into my eyes. The lighting was very dim, but I could see the sparkly pools that poets have long called the windows into the soul, and for an extended moment we quietly gazed at each other. Finally Theo spoke.

"If you don't believe in dating, how is a man supposed to get close to you?" he asked.

"He's not."

"Then why do I feel so close to you?"

"Chemistry, I told you that. Or maybe it's biology."

"And you don't ever react to your . . . your physical feelings?"

"I try not to," I said, but my voice didn't sound convincing, even to my own ears.

"I see. Let's test this theory of yours, shall we?" He leaned down until his lips were so close to mine, a magnetic pull began to take effect; to halt the kiss from happening would have taken a greater show of strength than I had in me. At the moment when our lips were about to touch, a horn honked, and Theo and I split apart immediately.

"Didn't think I'd desert you, did you?" Bob called from the open window of his car.

"You came all the way back here to give me a ride home?" I asked.

"Of course. Hop in."

Theo's hand grabbed mine. "There's a lot of unfinished business between us, Kylie," he said softly, more clearly visible now thanks to Bob's headlights.

I smiled. "Maybe," I said.

"For instance, this guy does not look like a friend of your great-aunts. He doesn't act like one, either."

"You're not jealous?" I asked incredulously.

"I guess I kind of am."

"I don't want you to be jealous. Heaven knows I'm not trying to play one of you against the other. Both of you are just friends."

He slowly ran a warm finger down my cheek. I was very aware of Bob watching this; I moved away a step and tried smiling again.

"Are you coming, Kylie?" Bob called.

"Good night," I told Theo and, crossing the street, got into Bob's car.

"Do you really want to go home?" Bob asked as he accelerated.

"I expect I'd better."

"Your great-aunts are pretty mad."

"They're mad in my house. I think I'd better be there to protect things."

"I don't believe they'd actually harm anything—"

"Neither do I, Bob. It was just a joke."

We were silent for a moment. Then he said, "I interrupted something between you and that veterinarian, didn't I?"

I looked at his profile and decided the truth was the best policy. "Yes, you did. But don't worry about it, because things were getting out of hand. As you know, I don't date—"

He took his eyes from the road. "What?"

I realized I'd never treated him to my anti-mating lecture, and while usually I could have worked up a decent head of steam on this subject, on this night I was feeling too subdued. I said, "I don't want to get married, so I generally don't date."

Bob laughed. "Well, since you're obviously not that attracted to me, then going out with me would hardly present much of a threat to your convictions, would it?"

"I guess not," I said as he pulled up outside my house. All the lights were on, so any chance of quietly putting off any confrontation until morning seemed unlikely.

Bob said, "I'll call you."

"No."

"Why not?"

"Because it just gets everyone all excited. I'm sorry, Bob, but you're right—I'm not attracted to you. Furthermore, I don't want to be attracted to you or anyone else. I also don't want to play games with your heart or with my own."

"Let me take care of my own heart," he said softly. "I may wear you down with my persistence."

I looked over my shoulder as I got out of his car. "Please, Bob, look for someone else, someone you can try to build a future with. You have a better than fifty-fifty chance of happiness. Don't waste your time on me. I'm sorry tonight turned out to be such a disaster.''

''Good night, Kylie,'' he said.

I had expected my aunts to be packing when I arrived home. Instead, they were seated on the sofa with both cats between them, presenting what appeared to be a united front.

Daisy's face was a little tear-streaked, and Prudence looked defiant. Though I felt awful that Daisy was suffering and that I was partly to blame, part of me felt the first stirring of relief: At least now they would go home and stop trying to manipulate my life. I tried to look contrite.

''Prue and I talked it over and decided you aren't to blame,'' Daisy said.

''That's right,'' Prue agreed, thereby extinguishing my hopes for a return to normalcy.

''It's that young man who was deceitful,'' Daisy said.

''Now wait a moment—''

''And as long as he stays away from here, I don't see any reason why Prue and I can't go on living with you until our house is ready for us.''

''Which should be early next week,'' Prudence said.

''Now wait a moment,'' I repeated. ''You know I love you both, but telling me who I may and may not see—''

"And we love you too," Daisy interrupted, and then she began crying again.

Prudence helped her sister stand. "Come along, Daisy. Let me tuck you into bed."

"It's just that I miss my little dog—"

"I know you do, dear. I'll make you a nice, warm glass of milk. . . ."

Their voices trailed off as the bedroom door closed behind them and I sat there with the two cats. Once again my great-aunts had had the last word.

Chapter Five

"*K*ylie," Carla Milton said over the phone. When I'd first met her, over eight months before when she'd come into Barton's looking for her dress with five of her friends who turned out to be the future matron of honor and bridesmaids, Carla's voice had been soft and rather sweet. It was now tinged with the raw edge of panic. "I know you don't know me well and that this really isn't your problem, but I finally got her to agree to ask you, and besides, there just isn't anyone else." After a dramatic pause, she added, "It's about my wedding."

Surprise. It would have taken a colder heart than mine not to assure Carla that I'd be happy to help in any way that I could, so I did.

"Then you must decide what we're going to do," she pleaded.

"Just slow down and explain your problem," I said.

93

"Remember how I told you my mother is driving me nuts? Now she's second-guessing the caterers at the country club. She wants to change the menu from chicken to beef. The wedding is only nine days away. How can she expect these people to change the menu?"

"She'll pay through the nose if she does," I said.

"I know. Who cares what we eat? Sometimes I think Felix—he's my fiancé—and I should just elope."

I personally thought that if a person insisted on getting married that this means of doing it far excelled any other, but, of course, I didn't say that. For one thing, I could see Madge marking down a rack of suits that was on the border of her department and mine, and I could just imagine how she'd like to report that little tidbit to Mrs. Sullivan. I said, "Carla, everything is going to turn out fine. I don't know what I can do about the chicken-versus-beef issue, but if you think it would help if I talked to your mother, then by all means I'll talk to your mother."

"Oh, that's not what I wanted to ask you. If Mother wants to pay to change the menu this late in the game, I don't care—I give up. The problem is Kipper."

"You mean those little fish? What are they called—herring?"

"No, I mean Felix's golden retriever, Kipper. I guess he ate a bunch of them when he was a pup—Oh, that doesn't matter. What matters is that Felix has decided that he wants Kipper to be the ring bearer."

A bark of laughter escaped before I could stop it. I

immediately turned serious and said, "Let me get this straight. Your fiancé wants his dog to deliver your ring?"

"That's right."

"And how do you feel about this?"

"Okay. I mean, it's absolutely the only thing Felix has asked out of this whole fiasco, so it seems only fair. What do you think?"

"I think your marriage may be one of the ones that makes it," I said wistfully, for I was very impressed with Carla's attitude. I added, "What does your mother think?"

"She's so upset, she's about to levitate. I reminded her it's an outside wedding, so what can Kipper hurt? I told her Felix and I practiced with Kipper and he did it perfectly every time. I told her Felix is going to be my husband and if she wants to make us both happy, she'll go along with it. She's agreed to go along with whatever you say."

"What!" This alarmed word caught Madge's attention. She took a few steps toward me. I smiled and said to Carla, through my teeth, "She is leaving this decision to me?"

"Yes. I know it's nuts, but that's the way things are around here right now."

I took a deep breath. I had the feeling that no matter what I said, I'd regret it, but since the idea of leaving this decision to me was preposterous to begin with, I'd say what Carla wanted to hear, because I liked her.

''Then I say that this is Felix's and your decision to make. If you both want the dog to carry the wedding ring, then have the dog carry the wedding ring. Just make sure you Velcro it to the pillow so he doesn't lose it in the grass.''

''Thank you, Kylie,'' she said. ''Thank you, thank you, thank you.''

As I hung up, I said, ''You're welcome, you're welcome, you're welcome . . . I hope.''

The next afternoon Sue Garvey came into the store, and after trying on eighteen dresses finally decided on the second one she'd seen, a relatively simple poly-satin gown with dolman sleeves and silver embroidered trim. The dress emphasized her small waist and hid her larger hips, and you couldn't ask much more of a dress than that.

She'd brought along her three bridesmaids, her mother, her soon-to-be mother-in-law, and her fiancé's aunt. The bridesmaids couldn't agree on a dress that would flatter all three of them for the simple reason, in my humble opinion, that such a dress does not exist. People do not and should not choose their wedding parties with concern for height and weight; however, fitting disparate figures in a single design is one of the true challenges facing a bridal consultant.

At last they all fell in love with an embossed ben-galine dress with a keyhole back. It even came in the right color, powder blue, and though only one of them actually looked good in the design, the others thought they did, which was just as good. The mother of the bride found a crepe/satin dress with a side drape, the mother-in-law-to-be ordered a lace sheath in a delicate petal pink, and the fiancé's aunt turned up her nose at everything in the store. As these things go, it was a rousing success, and after they left the store, I flopped down on my chair with a satisfied smile on my lips.

Madge said, "You certainly took long enough with them."

I frowned at her. "I took as long as it takes," I said at last.

"But two other customers got tired of waiting and left."

"Did it ever occur to you to come over here and help them?" I asked. This, of course, is what she should have done, what Barton's paid her to do. Many was the time I helped out in Madge's department, but the favor was never willingly repaid.

"I have a ton of my own work to do," she said, sniffing.

"I'm sure you do. But maybe next time you could just spend a moment or two finding out if they need to make an appointment."

"If you don't think I'm doing my job, then you should speak to Mrs. Sullivan," Madge said. "It's what I would do."

It's what you do do, no doubt, I thought, but I wasn't going to start ratting on Madge. My life was presently difficult enough without starting that, and besides, it was Mrs. Sullivan's job to keep an eye on her employees and talk to Madge herself.

Maybe I should run the whole store!

Saturday, I attended a small garden wedding. It was refreshing to witness a union made under the blue sky with garden flowers bobbing in the slight breeze and butterflies making unannounced visits. The bride and groom were both in their sixties, but the bride was as nervous as any young woman. I'd sold her the lovely ivory gown that complemented her figure and was rewarded when I heard her husband-to-be let out a protracted sigh as he caught sight of her walking down the aisle, her arm looped through her grown son's arm. It was enough to make even an antimarriage Scrooge like me feel a tear form in the corner of her eye.

Sunday's wedding was more traditional, though it did have a moment when it looked as though things might go awry. The groom was a young man wearing a very tight collar on his tuxedo. The church was small and crowded and, since the day outside was warm, stuffy. As the organ music began playing to announce the bride's arrival, I looked at the groom. I was always interested in how he reacted when he saw his intended approach, but this man looked next door to fainting, and I didn't believe it was because he was so overwhelmed with the vision of loveliness who was slowly walking down the aisle toward him.

Frantically, but trying hard not to make a fuss, I excused myself and found the church official, who helped me open a few windows and doors to create cross ventilation. I think we revived the man seconds before he was ready to keel over on top of his wife-to-be, which would have made my day more interesting but would no doubt have ruined it for everyone else.

Other than that, the most exciting things that happened that weekend were the calories I consumed for breakfast as Great-Aunt Daisy buried her sorrow by stuffing me full of food.

The next week was the week before Carla's wedding, or the "Milton Countdown," as I tagged it. Every day Carla called with a new dilemma or a new question, and every day I tried my best to do what I could for her. I'd met her mother only once, and she'd seemed reasonable enough; obviously the impending wedding was taking its toll on the poor woman.

Toward the last of the week Amanda Brighton came into the store with her matron of honor, who was every bit as striking as Amanda—tall, blond, built like a model. I thought about this wedding and what the photographs would look like with Theo standing beside Mike (I assumed Theo would stand beside Mike, just as I assumed Mike would be a knockout like his bride-to-be.) We found Marie—the blonde—a wraparound fuchsia dress with lace trim. To no one's surprise but her own, she looked gorgeous.

As I wrote up the order form for Marie's dress, I

asked Amanda, "How is Theo?" I tried to sound very casual, as though I were being nothing more than polite.

"He's okay," she answered. "Working very hard at his practice, of course, but he loves all those animals, says he doesn't even consider it work." She paused for a second and added, "Mike and I took Theo to dinner last night. I don't know how you're doing it, Kylie, but you sure have my big brother coming and going."

I'm afraid my gaze flew up to her face. "What do you mean?"

"Is *this* the woman Theo keeps talking about?" Marie asked as she wrote the deposit check.

"This is her."

Marie looked at me with raised eyebrows. I felt as though I were turning bright red, but I plastered a smile on my face and laughed. "Theo is just pulling your leg."

"Theo invented the word cool," Marie said. "I've been Amanda's best friend since grade school; I hate to admit the years I wasted trying to get Theo to notice me."

One: I was not surprised any female would try to get Theo Brighton to notice her. Two: How could any male not notice Marie?

"Is it true you won't date him?" Amanda asked.

"I just don't date, period," I said. "Of course, it has nothing to do with him."

"Hm—" Amanda said.

Marie said, "You're nuts. He's successful, he's gorgeous, and, to top it all, he's nice."

Those things were all true. There hadn't been a moment that went by since the second our lips had been about to promise what our minds were too obstinate to even think about that I hadn't thought of him. I knew how he smelled and how he looked and how tall he was. I knew about the warmth that radiated from his muscular body, about the shape of his hands and the gentleness he used when examining a small animal in need.

More than that, I knew the way I felt when I saw him, the way his mouth curved when he saw me. I hadn't felt this way since Johnny, and that scared me, not only because I was afraid of being hurt again if I let my heart rule my decisions, but also because I wasn't sure if my feelings were for Theo or were some kind of latent mixed-up residual feelings for Johnny.

Marie was staring at me. As she handed me the check, she said, "Theo is a wonderful man. If he ever looked my way, I'd snap him up in a big hurry, believe you me."

I took her check and handed her a receipt. "It was so nice meeting you," I said. She smiled a smile that said she knew what I meant even though I felt like a child lost in the fog.

There was a reason for this. After two years of no men in my life, I suddenly found myself thinking about three. Bob Oliveras surfaced in my thoughts now and again as a safe choice for a long-time companion. It was true we weren't soulmates, but wasn't that his main attraction? It would be cheating him because I would never love him or marry him, but from my point of view, Bob was a safe bet.

Then there was Johnny. I'd managed to cast him into the black oblivion he deserved until my mother asked about him; the fact that I'd taken her comments to heart made me doubt my convictions. Would I be thinking about him this much if I didn't harbor old feelings? Could I possibly still love the jerk?

And most of all there was Theo, the man who made my insides feel funny, the man I was determined to stay away from but the one I kept encountering with increasingly strong feelings that reawakened a lot of fears of vulnerability. I'd told him it was biology, chemistry, whatever a person wants to call it when a man and a woman feel something special for each other. Did it matter what name we gave it?

Three men, two great-aunts, one missing father. No wonder I felt confused.

The Friday night before the Milton wedding, as I sat at my desk in the living room and Prudence and Daisy put the finishing touches on their special pot roast, I received another call from Carla. I'd been going through my mail, but when I heard Carla's voice, I put it aside.

"It's my mother," she groaned.

"Why aren't you at your rehearsal dinner?" I asked.

"I am. Mother is making more noise about Kipper. Have you seen the weather outside?"

Along about Wednesday, I'd given up trying to make sense of Carla's train of thought, so I said, "It's a little breezy, that's all. What's the dog got to do with the weather?"

"*Everything,* according to Mother. She says that winds scare a dog. She says that Kipper will start biting people."

"Has Kipper ever bitten anyone before?" I asked, unconsciously looking at the faint scar on my finger put there by the late Mr. Fu.

"Of course not. Felix is getting really tired of this."

I didn't blame Felix.

"Mother wants my cousin's son Kevin to carry the ring. That's why she's making such a fuss."

"Oh." I didn't say anything else, because for the life of me I wasn't sure what I could possibly do to help. After a few seconds' pause I finally added, "Carla, stand up to your mother. Stand up for Felix." I sounded as though I were about to burst into a chorus of "Stand By Your Man," so I stopped talking.

"You're right," she said. "I'll tell her you said so."

"No, don't do that—" I intoned, but the line was dead.

Carla had finally infused me with the same haunting premonition she'd been feeling, only now I dreaded that whatever horrible thing was going to happen would somehow be my fault!

"Dinner's almost ready," Daisy called from the kitchen. "Wash up, Kylie."

Knowing I would be forever a small child in her mind, a child with mud-stained hands and jelly-smeared lips, I didn't tell her that I was already as clean as the proverbial whistle. I went back to my mail instead. There on the bottom was a letter with hand-writing so familiar and yet so much a part of the past that I felt all the breath whisk out of my lungs.

I opened the envelope with shaking fingers and read the short note:

Kylie—

Can you ever forgive me? Cold feet, cruel heart, name it what you will, but I want to make it up to you. I want to mend fences. I still love you. I'll call you soon.

Johnny

I found myself standing, staring down at the of-fending paper. How dare the man waltz back into my life after what he'd done? Did he honestly think a few clever words masquerading as an apology were going to cut it with me? Sitting back down at the desk, I picked up the phone receiver and dialed my mother's number, but then I hung up before it rang.

What could she do to help? What could anyone do?

All I knew with burning certainty was that I didn't want to see Johnny Page again. I didn't want to hear his words or see his face. I'd protected my heart from men like him, and here was the real thing, my own personal prototype of a capital A-One Jerk, back in town to do . . . back to do what?

I read the note again. *I still love you,* he wrote. I found I had stood again—in fact, that I had begun pacing as though something in me said to run and something else said, *No, come back.*

Into the midst of this profound inner turmoil came my great-aunt's voice, informing me that dinner was on the table. I folded the letter, which I found still grasped in my hand, and put it in the desk drawer along with the envelope.

Through no fault of the cook or the recipe, the special pot roast tasted like dead leaves. My great-aunts talked about their house and how the painters had said they'd need a little longer, as the wallpaper stripping wasn't coming along so well in the bathroom, but even that didn't faze me. The little black cat with the big tummy was busy crunching a bowl of some kind of dry cat food, and it was her/him I watched while the rest of the world kind of slipped by.

"What in the daylights is wrong with you, Kylie?" Prudence demanded. I saw that I now had a plate before me on which resided a piece of peach pie.

"I'm tired," I said. "I'll get some extra rest to-night."

The phone rang, which startled the black cat. It ran back out into the living room, where it resumed crouching under the sofa while Daisy answered the phone.

"It's for you, Kylie," she called.

I froze. What if it was Johnny?

"It's Bob Oliveras," she added. "Come on, dear, come to the phone."

I shook my head and spoke. My voice sounded rusty. "Tell him I'll speak to him tomorrow or the next day."

"Now, Kylie," Prudence said. "You mustn't play *too* hard to get, not at your age."

I must have cast her a look that said exactly how I felt about that statement, for she's the one who scooted out to the phone and mumbled something into the receiver. The rest of the night, they treated me like a child with a short temper, which was fine with me.

I awoke Saturday morning knowing I'd dreamed of Johnny. As I drifted between slumber and full wakefulness, I imagined what he might look like now. He'd still be dashing; two years wasn't long enough to change a thirty-year-old man too much. He'd still have a small cleft in his chin, still have wavy dark hair, still have those bottomless brown eyes that had once absorbed every morsel of my independence.

I rolled over and shut my eyes. I tried not to think, but for the first time in two years I began to remember some of the good times: The rides in his car, the picnic out at the abandoned lighthouse, the late nights spent with three rented movies and tubs of popcorn. I recalled the plans we'd made, the kisses we'd shared, the kind words he'd spoken when I was sick.

No! When he called, I'd tell him he was history, that I didn't want his explanations; I didn't need them or him. I'd tell him it was too late to mend fences.

By late Saturday afternoon I'd fielded two more frantic calls from Carla. As her mother (or the weatherman) had predicted, the wind had continued to rise, but after ascertaining that it was too late to move the ceremony inside, I reminded her that the wind often dropped at night and not to worry.

I asked her what was the worst thing that could happen—it was an old trick my father had taught me when I was a child. Imagine the worst scenario. If you can cope with it, then stop worrying. Carla imagined such awful things that I immediately regretted trying the ploy with her.

Since the wedding was extremely formal even though the service was to be held outside, I dressed with special care. I chose a floor-length blue chiffon skirt and topped it with an asymmetrical silk top covered with beads, pearls, and sequins that formed an all-over floral design. As I slipped on my blue pumps, it occurred to me that the one good thing about the wind, which hadn't dropped, was that it would dry the grass and no dyed silk shoes would bleed.

My great-aunts were most impressed by my appearance, which I found endearing. "Don't wait up," I told them. "It promises to be a late evening."

"But, Kylie, why is your beautiful hair all tucked back?" Daisy asked.

"Because of the wind, dear. And because I'm going to be working, you know, and I don't want to bother with my hair."

"I've never heard of a wedding in the dark," Prudence said with pursed lips. "Sounds stupid to me."

I kissed them both good-bye and left.

I was early, of course, but even so, the country club was almost ready. It sat in a small valley nestled in among redwood trees; golf-course greens rolled gently away in three directions. The club itself was single story with a giant cement patio and a pool off to the side. I surveyed the scene before I went to find Carla.

The torches—I had no idea which kind they were—were enclosed but sat atop long poles. They'd been set up on the far side of the chairs, forming a border between the wedding party and the acres of golf course. Hundreds of chairs were set up too. The altar was ringed with more lanterns and formed a backdrop between the club and the rolling greens; it was decorated to within an inch of its life with flowers. They must have been secured with Super Glue because none of them blew away, and the wind had come up to the point where it wouldn't have surprised me if they did.

Even some of the metal chairs were beginning to bang into one another.

This was all easy to see because it wasn't yet totally dark, and besides, I could see several floodlights, which I assumed would be turned off when the lanterns were lit.

As I walked inside the club, I peeked into the huge reception area. It, too, was decorated lavishly. Several waiters and waitresses were combing the room, getting it ready for the moment when the perishable food would be set out on the candlelit tables. Smaller round tables were also candlelit or would be once the lights went out. I saw several little candy cups but didn't take the time to see whether the Jordan almonds had made it through the final cut.

Carla was in the women's dressing room. Surrounded by friends, family, and gold golfing trophies, which I assumed belonged to the club members, she looked like an actress about to make a stage debut, which in a way was exactly what she was. The dress hung on a portable rack along with the bridesmaids' dresses, flouncy affairs of mint-green organza. I saw the stack of hats the bridesmaids were supposed to wear, and the first bit of trepidation nibbled at the back of my neck. How would we keep all those hats in place?

The next hour was filled with a blaze of activity. As Carla's mother buzzed around the room, supervising everyone and making things far more tense than they needed to be, I helped Carla with her gown. Once we had her buttoned in place, I helped the bridesmaids get themselves all pulled together. We used an entire box of bobby pins to anchor the hats, taking special care with Carla's, and even though her mother kept insisting that they'd all be airborne, I thought we'd done a pretty good job.

Once the women were almost finished, I knocked on the door of the men's changing room and found Felix. His attendants had left to seat the wedding guests, and he seemed happy to see me. The man looked as though he could use a stiff drink, or maybe what he really needed was for the ceremony to be over.

I also met Kipper, the ring bearer, a golden retriever with a bright-red collar. Kipper sat beside Felix's legs with a good-natured smile on his attractive face. Felix showed me the small velvet pillow the wedding ring was attached to with a piece of Velcro as I had suggested.

The last time I'd seen the ring, it had been on Carla's hand. It was composed of several huge diamonds all stacked up next to one another. I wasn't a good judge of jewelry prices, but that ring looked terribly expensive. I said, "Isn't this Carla's engagement ring? I assumed the dog would be carrying a simple gold band."

"She didn't want a band," Felix said. "She said this thing is so big, it practically buries her first knuckle, so we agreed that this ring would serve as both an engagement ring and as a wedding band.''

"So the dog is going to carry this ring?" I realized that asking him that again made me sound very dense, but I was still a little flabbergasted.

He nodded.

I patted the dog on his head and decided I'd watch to see where he dropped the velvet pillow if the wind should rouse him into a fit of frenzied biting.

Felix's father was entering the room as I left. "Be sure to brush the dog hair off of Felix's trousers," I told the older man, who laughed and slapped his son on the back.

On my way to the women's dressing room, I peeked outside. Almost every chair was filled, and the country-club workers were starting to light the hurricane lamps; I hoped the name signified that they'd hold up to the wind, which looked to be gusting up to twenty miles per hour. I wished I'd taken Carla's advice and brought a sweater. At least one good thing was certain: No mosquito could make headway in a wind like this.

I went back in to see how Carla was doing. She tried smiling and actually pulled it off when someone came and claimed her mother to be seated. Mrs. Milton hugged her daughter, told her she looked beautiful, reiterated her concerns about Kipper and the hats and the wind and the Jordan almonds, then began crying as she was dragged away. As the bridesmaids made their way out to the area they'd stand in before they walked down the aisle in front of Carla, I took the bride's clammy hands.

"You look wonderful," I told her.

"Thanks. I think I should cancel this whole thing, though. Too much can go wrong—"

"Don't you love Felix?"

"Of course I love Felix," she whispered. "He didn't want a big wedding, you know. I didn't, either. Oh, I mean at first I did when it all sounded like a fairy tale, but now that the reality has hit—"

I smiled. "Do you want to know what Felix asked me to tell you?"

"You saw him!"

"Just a few minutes ago. He looked very handsome, though I imagine there's going to be a few gold hairs on his pants. He said to tell you to keep your chin up and your head down. He says he loves you."

Carla's lips trembled, and her eyes grew huge and watery.

"Don't you dare cry and smudge that makeup," I said.

That made her laugh.

At last it was time for Carla's big entrance. As her father waited, I straightened out the long, transparent train. I adjusted the pleats, tucked a stray lock of hair up into her hat, wished her good luck, and hurried to my seat.

The floodlights had been turned off so the scene was lit only by the torches. Enclosed and burning gas, the flames didn't flicker and dance, but they were an amber color and helped create the illusion of a primitive scene, a wildly romantic one. The guests were all caught up in the magic of the hour, and we sat still and silent and expectant.

Considering the wind and the unusual setting, things started out so well. As I sat down, the last bridesmaid/usher combination turned and divided at the makeshift altar. The piano music stopped, there was a moment of anticipatory silence, and then the bridal march began. I rose as everyone else did. Carla looked perfect—except that one hand held the hat in place. Her skirt, so heavy with the beads, stayed right down around her legs as it was supposed to. As per my habit, I turned my attention to the groom.

Felix's face was filled with wonder as his bride approached. Something in my heart and throat caught at the sight of him, and for the first time it occurred to me that the real reason I watched the groom was that part of me never quite believed he'd be there; part of me always expected that he'd have had a change of mind and fled, leaving a bewildered bride—the bride I'd helped dress, the bride I'd helped prepare for this fantasy called marriage—leaving her high and dry and brokenhearted as I myself had once been.

But Felix was there, and as I watched his face as Carla approached, I mused that all the thousands upon thousands of dollars' worth of wedding trappings were immaterial because of what was on his face and was undoubtedly reflected in her eyes. I scooted over a bit and lowered my gaze and saw that Kipper sat still and polite, the little pillow firmly clenched in his jaws.

It was about then that there was an especially strong gust of wind. One by one, like dominoes, the torches fell, and as they did, probably as a safety precaution, they were extinguished. The end effect was that within the space of thirty seconds, every torch but one was out, and the wedding was plunged into darkness.

The piano music stopped at once, and the only noise that anyone heard for a time was the wind as it twisted its way through the small valley. Finally a man coughed, and then voices followed.

Because of the one remaining burning torch, which was ironically placed closest to the altar, it wasn't totally dark. Everyone could see the panic on Felix's face and the nervous glances and whispers exchanged among the bridesmaids. Trapped somewhere between the altar and the country-club doors would be Carla. Actually, when you knew where to look, you could see the glimmer of her bead-and-crystal-studded gown. I hoped her innate good humor would kick in and keep her sensible until the country-club people got the situation under control.

The woman next to me said, "People nowadays can't just have normal weddings anymore. First they invite us here in the dead of night, and then they make us sit outside in this chilly wind, and now this! Do you suppose the lights were supposed to go off?"

About then, a hail of male voices barking orders preceded half the floodlights switching on; there was a general sigh of relief from participants and spectators alike. I looked around until I could see Carla. She was clinging to her father's arm, but there was a smile on her face.

As I turned from looking at her, I caught a glimpse of another familiar face—Theo Brighton. He didn't see me, and for a moment I greedily absorbed his profile. It occurred to me how little time we'd spent together and that my feelings were actually way too strong, considering how little I knew about him. Did that confirm that I was using him as a Johnny Page substitute, or did it mean that I was on the verge of falling in love with Theo? Or maybe it meant I wasn't getting enough sleep and I needed to stop thinking so much. At any rate, Carla had said that everyone in the world would be at the wedding. From my point of view, she was right.

The piano music started again. I tore my gaze from Theo and looked at the altar. Felix, his best man, the ushers, and Kipper all stood waiting. If Carla and her father walked a little faster, who could blame them, but at least Carla's mother would have to admit that Kipper had conducted himself with canine aplomb.

Carla finally reached her destination. The usual words were spoken between the minister and the parents, and Carla took Felix's hand. The service continued, and except for that one moment of darkness, it looked as though things were going to come off without a hitch when all of a sudden another gust of wind swept through the valley.

The last standing torch gave up. As the women's hands all flew to anchor their hats and skirts from the invading gust, I watched in heart-stopping suspense as the last burning torch fell within a foot of the farthermost usher from the groom; the man jumped nimbly aside as a cry of alarm escaped his lips.

I saw Felix look down to check his dog. His head snapped up immediately; then he turned and scanned the crowd. He turned back to Carla, whispered something in her ear, then gazed out beyond the altar.

My eyes followed his. Kipper had finally had it. There was just enough light to see his golden rump disappearing over the greens, out of sight.

Chapter Six

I don't think the majority of the crowd had any idea exactly why Kipper's desertion raised such an immediate and anguished search. Within minutes all the floodlights were on. Felix and his ushers and his parents all roamed the immediate area, their eyes downcast as they looked for the velvet pillow and its expensive cargo, their voices raised as they pleaded with Kipper to come back. Carla's mother mercifully fell into some kind of stupor, and though I saw a woman fanning her face with a program—*In this wind, someone is fanning her?* I thought—at least she was spared the half hour where everything stopped as an all-points bulletin was spread across the valley: Be on the lookout for a gold dog carrying a diamond ring.

I spent the time cowering behind people so Theo wouldn't inadvertently see me. I wasn't sure why I acted so cowardly, whether it was seeing him on the heels of receiving the disquieting letter from Johnny or because my own emotions seemed too fragile, but at any rate I put off the moment when I'd feel my heart thump down to my knees as his lips formed a smile.

The dog finally returned. He no longer carried the pillow with the ring, but he did look as though the long run had been enjoyable and, panting, washed Felix's hand. I imagined the man was about ready to make the dog into a throw rug.

Most of the guests had stood and meandered about during this interval, but the dog's return seemed to signal an unspoken command to return to their seats. Felix spoke with Carla; then he stood on the altar in front of the minister until we were all seated and quiet.

"Thank you for your patience," he said. "I know you're all windblown and probably getting kind of tired, and Carla and I appreciate your forbearance. We've had a small mishap, but the purpose of this evening remains the same—Carla and I love each other and want to be married here, in front of our family and our friends."

I saw Carla reach down and unbuckle Kipper's red collar. She handed it to Felix and said, "You'll have to use this as a token of your love until your dog brings back my ring."

A moment of stunned silence was followed by a slow wave of laughter. I couldn't see Mrs. Milton's face; no doubt it was not quite as amused as her daughter's, which was a shame. I thought she should have been very proud.

The ceremony continued. I found myself thinking that Carla was getting a good man and that they truly deserved each other, for she beamed as Felix looped the silly collar over her arm. No one would ever know by looking at her that several thousand dollars of diamonds were lost somewhere out on the greens.

I was aware that a few young men armed with flashlights combed the golf course, but other than that, the rest of the wedding proceeded in a more traditional way. Carla told me that she didn't want to keep everyone waiting while she and Felix had hundreds of photographs taken, so she had the photographer take a modest number while people went inside and warmed up after being subjected to the cool wind for almost an hour. I helped make sure the dress—well, the whole bride and all her attendants—looked good for the photos so they'd be a credit to Barton's bridal department for all eternity. After they left to form the receiving line, I turned right into Theo's chest.

"Been avoiding me?" he asked.

THUMP. I said, "Of course not. What are you doing here?"

"I went to school with Felix."

"You went to school with half this town."

"If half the town is composed of thirty-year-olds, then I suppose you're right. Are you working?"

"Not anymore." I spared a second to wonder what would happen to my job if the ring weren't found. Would Carla's mother recall that it was I who had said let the dog have a go at carrying it?

"I don't suppose you have the inside scoop on what happened out there tonight. Besides the dog running away, I mean. Rumor has it the animal was carrying Carla's wedding ring."

"For once rumor is right on target," I said and explained what I knew. Theo tried to keep from laughing, but besides the financial loss, the whole thing did have its humor, and I didn't blame him when he lost the battle with decorum and let out a hearty chuckle or two.

Eventually we made it through the receiving line. It was eleven o'clock at night by now, and I was getting very tired. It was by far the latest wedding I'd ever attended. Yawning, I came face-to-face with Mr. and Mrs. Milton. I saw Mrs. Milton's eyebrows raise when she saw me, but I guess her good manners kept her from telling me exactly how she felt about me.

"I know that you don't like champagne," Theo said. "How about a glass of punch?"

"Thank you. I'd love one."

He got me the punch, and we sat for a while and chatted. I told him I'd met Marie, and he smiled. "She's a cute kid," he said.

"She is not a kid," I told him.

"She is to me. I can't look at Marie the woman

without seeing Marie the child, and that comes complete with a recollection of her and Amanda dressed up in my mother's clothes. Marie had red lipstick smeared from one end of her mouth to the other.''

''Well, in case you haven't noticed, Marie has finally mastered the art of applying lipstick,'' I said dryly.

He laughed. ''I noticed. I'm not blind, just not interested.''

Why did that declaration make me feel so good, and why did I have the distinct feeling that he knew it did?

''Do you want to dance?'' he asked.

I hesitated.

''I promise I won't drag you off on a date or try to marry you. We'll just move around to the music and pretend we're strangers. How about it?''

''How can a girl refuse an offer like that?'' I asked.

The moment I stepped into the circle of his arms, it felt like coming home. He was very warm and very strong; even his heartbeat seemed to rattle my cheek as I momentarily lost myself and rested my head against his chest. I closed my eyes and swallowed and knew I was in deep water.

His hand closed on mine. His other hand moved very slowly up and down my back, urging me closer, and I went. I'd lost myself before, and I was on the verge of losing myself again when common sense made me open my eyes and take a step away from him.

Around us, other dancers continued their moves, but Theo and I stood still, staring into each other's eyes.

"Kylie—" he said at last.

I turned and made my way through the dancers to our table, where I picked up my bag. I turned when I felt warm hands on my arms.

"Don't run away from me," he pleaded.

"I have to," I said as I turned to face him.

"You mean you want to."

"No, I have to because I don't want to."

He nodded as though I made sense.

Into this highly charged scene came the sound of Carla hailing me. "Kylie, Kylie," she called joyfully, all the strain and craziness gone now that the ceremony was over. I envied her.

Theo dropped his hands, but he stayed facing me as I turned to greet Carla.

"Where have you been hiding?" she demanded. She waved her hand, and I noticed the red collar dangling just below her elbow. "Never mind, I want you to meet one of Felix's friends. He just got into town today, and when he saw you, he asked me to introduce you. . . ."

I don't know what else she said because just then I saw who was standing behind her. He came a few steps closer.

His hair was slightly longer, and his skin was tanned a becoming brown. His dark eyes scanned my face, at first with trepidation but almost instantly with an air of self-assurance that did more to alarm me than any words he could have spoken. When he smiled, I felt an odd combination of familiarity and strangeness. I also felt as though the room were spinning one way and my head was spinning the other. *He was supposed to call!* I thought frantically. *I wasn't supposed to have to face him without warning!*

"This is Johnny Page," Carla said.

Johnny took one of my limp hands and advanced the charade by saying, "How very nice to meet you!"

I didn't know what to say. I felt Theo's eyes on me. All I knew for sure was that I had to get out of there. Jerking my hand away, I mumbled something, anything, and fled.

I heard footsteps behind me as I made my way through the room; then I was stopped by the heavy wooden doors. Before I could yank one of them open, a man pushed from the outside. I barely noticed the look of surprise that crossed his face as I darted under his arm and out into the windblown night.

I heard mumbled apologies behind me as whoever pursued me ran into the man with the door. And then my arm was grasped from behind, and I whirled around to face Johnny.

But it was Theo who stood there, not Johnny, Theo who wrapped his strong arm around my trembling shoulders, Theo who started walking again, half carrying me with him.

"My car is in the other direction," I protested.

"You can't drive in the condition you're in." He

opened the door and deposited me on the front seat of a Jeep without a top.

"This isn't your car—"

"I have two." He got in behind the wheel and started the engine. The last thing I saw as he pulled away from the country club was Johnny standing by the doors, searching the parking lot, looking for me. As far as I could tell, he didn't look twice at the Jeep.

"I don't want to go home," I mumbled. Johnny must know where I lived if he'd written me a letter. If he was crazy enough to pull a stunt like the one he'd just pulled, he was crazy enough to go to my house at midnight. Let him wake my great-aunts; they'd love to give him a piece of their mind.

I saw Theo glance in my direction. "Where do you want to go?" he asked.

"I don't care." I closed my eyes and tried not to think. It was hopeless, so I opened my eyes again and said, "This thing needs shock absorbers."

"So do you. When Carla introduced that man, you looked as though you'd seen a ghost."

"That's how I felt," I admitted.

"Who is he?"

"I don't want to talk about him." For the first time I noticed we'd left the city limits and were traveling down a dark road. "Where are we?"

"On the way to my place."

"What?"

"Well, you didn't want to go home, and you said

you didn't care where you went, and I'm too tired to go sit in some bar, which is about the only thing in Cypress Bay that's open this time of night, unless you want to count the grocery store, which I don't. Is that okay with you?''

There was a note of sarcasm in his voice that was new to me. I didn't blame him one bit, however, for being annoyed with the way I was acting, so I said, ''Sure. Why not?''

He lived down a twisty little dirt road that erupted suddenly into a clearing. The house lights were off, but two porch lights blazed gallantly in the dark so I could see a little of his yard. I heard barking.

The barking was explained when Theo got out of the Jeep and fought his way around to my door through a sea of dogs. Standing up in the Jeep, I asked, ''Are they all yours?''

''Every one of them,'' he said. He seemed to realize then how I was dressed. ''I can lock them up while we get you to the house, or we can do this.'' With that, he tugged on my hand until I fell toward him; then he slung me over his shoulder. My head was hanging down his back. I started laughing as one of the dogs—it looked like a collie mix—licked my nose.

''Nice to hear you laughing,'' Theo said as he climbed the stairs onto a redwood deck. I heard him put a key into a lock and then push the door open. Once we were inside, he leaned down and set me on my feet. He straightened up and looked down at me.

He flipped on the light, and though I was curious to look around the house, for the moment I was held in place by the hazel of his eyes.

He said, "I don't know about you, but I'm starving."

As Theo disappeared into the kitchen to "scrounge" for food—his word, not mine—I went around the downstairs floor of the house, investigating. There were still packing boxes piled in the corners, but the main living area had been cleared. It was a huge place that looked as though it might have been at one time a hunter's retreat. I got this impression not only from the fireplace, which was large enough to hold a poker party in, but also from the various animal heads fastened to the walls.

"Did you shoot all these poor little woodland creatures?" I asked.

"Nope," he called. "I only rent the place. I'm a veterinarian, you know. I save animals; I don't kill them."

"Then how do you stand all these glassy eyes looking down at you all the time?"

By this time I'd worked my way into the kitchen. Theo had taken off his jacket and rolled up his sleeves. He wore a pair of bright-blue suspenders over his white shirt and stood in front of the stove scrambling eggs.

"I try to ignore them," he called over his shoulder. "Hey, butter that toast, will you?" he asked as he caught sight of me in the doorway.

I got to the toaster just as it spat two pieces of bread halfway across the counter.

"How many dogs do you have?" I asked as I buttered the bread.

"Four. Wait, five."

"Are they all huge?"

"No. There were a couple of runts in the pack, but they were down near the ground and you couldn't see them."

"So how do you always look so immaculate if they attack you coming and going?"

"They obey word commands."

"Right."

"When I want them to. When there isn't a beautiful woman I want to carry into the house."

Our eyes met, but I turned away. "I'll set the table," I said.

He pointed at a drawer, and I got him some silverware and, from the open shelf against the wall, a plate. "Aren't you having any?" he asked.

"I'm not hungry." I sat down at the big wooden chopping-block table. It was right next to floor-to-ceiling windows, but as it was dark outside, I had no idea what the kitchen overlooked. Theo handed me a steaming mug of coffee and pointed at the sugar bowl. "Cream?"

"No, thanks." I wrapped my hands around the mug and watched him flit about the kitchen with ease. As upset as I'd been at the country club, it was incredible to me that I could feel so relaxed now. Actually, it was more than that. I felt comfortable in a way I'd never experienced. I wondered if it was the house, all dark wood and high ceilings and masculine trappings. And then I wondered if it was Theo.

Finally, when Theo had put enough food on the table to feed a small army, he sat down beside me. He handed me a fork and a knife and a plate, and though I had fully intended just to keep him company, I found myself eating instead and before long had polished off my share of the impromptu meal.

"That was delicious. No wonder you don't want to get married. What do you need a woman for?"

He looked into my eyes and said, "There are a few things it's much nicer to do with a woman."

I glanced at the wall clock and saw that it was two in the morning. "Good heavens, look at the time."

"Who is he?" Theo asked.

I sighed heavily. "Johnny Page."

"I know that. What I don't know is who he is to you."

I looked down at the last remnants of egg on my plate and tried to formulate the right words. My mind was a jumbled blank, which was not only a mixed metaphor but accurately described the way I felt.

Theo sat back in his chair. "Do you know what I see when I look at you?" he asked.

"I'm afraid to know," I muttered.

"Since you asked so nicely, I'll tell you. I see a

very competent young woman as well as a very pretty one. But past the smart brain and the brown eyes and the heart-shaped face and the pearly skin, I see a woman who was hurt, maybe more than once. I see a woman who has pulled in the drawbridge.''

I started to stand, but his hand caught my wrist. He released me at once, but then he said, ''Let me finish.''

So I sat.

''I like my metaphor, so I'll expand on it,'' he continued. ''All is not peaceful in the castle. True, pulling up the drawbridge has made it so the princess is safe from any marauding dragons, but she's also out of reach of her Prince Charming.''

''Maybe she doesn't want a Prince Charming,'' I said.

''That's where the real trouble lies. She does want a Prince Charming. She doesn't want the old-fashioned kind who charges in on a white horse and whisks her away from all her troubles. She wants the kind who knocks on the door, the kind who sharpens his own lance, the kind who wants her to help him plant water lilies in the royal moat. She needs the kind of Prince Charming who needs her to adore him the way he adores her.''

Neither one of us spoke. In the silence we heard the dogs padding around the deck and the tick of the wall clock as it counted off time.

Finally I said, ''The princess knows what she's doing.''

"And this Johnny fellow, is he a former Prince Charming?"

I nodded. I felt tears forming in my eyes and hastily wiped them away. I did not want to cry, especially about Johnny Page, in front of Theo. I said, "To pay for my meal, I'll satisfy your curiosity. Johnny is the man I was supposed to marry. He backed out as I stood waiting to march down the aisle. He left without talking to me; he just left a dumb note. There, are you satisfied?"

He put his finger under my chin and raised my face until our eyes met. "You know I wasn't asking out of idle curiosity."

"I know," I admitted, feeling guilty and awful.

"And besides, that wasn't what the meal cost. The going price for scrambled eggs and toast these days is a kiss. How about it? Do you want to pay now, or do you want to run a check?"

I was powerless to withstand him. He didn't make a move toward me, just sat there staring at me. It was I who gravitated toward him, once again as though obeying a magnetic force. Our lips met. I was jolted and withdrew, but within a heartbeat was back.

The kiss should have lasted only as long as it takes for a confused woman to realize she's about to make the same mistake she's made before. Intellectually I knew I should pull away, but emotionally or physically or whatever you want to call it, I was glued to Theo. I felt his fingers touch my cheek so gently it was like the fluttering wings of a moth. The caress grew more assured as his fingers trailed down my neck, curved around my chin. I felt his knee press against mine, felt the heat of his body so close, so close.

He drew away, and we peered into each other's eyes, and then his lips were on mine again, and this time the kisses were greedy and hungry. He set little fires along my neck, up my cheek, across my brow as I ran my fingers through his hair and across his broad shoulders.

It was the first time in two years that I'd kissed a man, been held by one with tenderness and caring. It was the first time in years that I'd let my emotions fly, and I felt like an empty bird cage awaiting the return of the canary, eager for its return but a little sad at the thought of caging something so beautiful.

Eventually we needed a moment apart, and that's when my brain finally spoke loud enough to be heard. "Theo, we have to stop. I'm so confused. . . ."

"I know you are," he said huskily.

"I don't know—"

"I'll tell you what I know," he said as he nibbled on my ear. "I know you need to face this Johnny Page and put the past away, because it's beginning to interfere with my pursuit of the future."

With tremendous effort I pushed myself away. "You said you didn't believe in marriage."

"Brace yourself," he grumbled. "I lied."

"But you're making it sound as though the only problem is that I must choose whom I love and want to spend my life with when that's not the issue at all. I don't want any man—''

Impatiently he interrupted me. ''You've been lying to yourself so long, you wouldn't know your true feelings if they sneaked up and pinched you.''

I tried to sputter some indignant remark, but I suspected his words held at least a grain of truth, though I wasn't ready to admit it to myself, let alone to him, just yet. I said, ''I don't—''

He stood abruptly. ''I'm about to give up on you, Kylie Armstrong. If you still love Johnny, so be it. Just find out for sure, will you? And do me one more favor—start being honest with yourself. Now come on, darling, I'm taking you home.''

Chapter Seven

*I*s it any wonder I dreamed that night of castles and dragons and knights in shining armor or that I awoke late and grumpy and in a sour mood? I lay in bed for quite a while, listening to the vacuum as Daisy cleaned the floors. I wanted my great-aunts to go away, but in all fairness I more or less wanted the whole world to go away as well.

The trouble with people like Theo Brighton was that they thought they had all the answers. Theo barely knew me, and yet he pretended he could see deep down into my soul and figure me out better than I could figure myself out. This was what was wrong with men, I decided as I staggered into the shower.

But was he right? As I lathered myself with soap, I relived the night before. In fact, it seemed that every moment I'd ever spent with him or near him crowded into my mind until I was filled with impressions the way a kaleidoscope is filled with colorful beads of glass. Did I need to shift the focus to see what really filled my heart? Didn't I already know? Hadn't I since the minute I found out Theo was Amanda's brother and not her husband? Wasn't the only thing that kept me from him my own fear? Or was Johnny Page part of the equation?

Wait a second, I thought as I wore the soap down to a slippery sliver. *What about all my ideals? What about my conviction that marriage is a fifty-fifty proposition at best?*

A tiny little voice spoke through the bubbles in my head: *If it is fifty-fifty and you've been next door to committing it once and got burned, then doesn't that mean your chances are better the next time?*

Be quiet, I told myself. *That's crazy. It's not the same thing at all. Think about something else.*

The only other thought that presented itself for my perusal was of my great-aunts, who had been with me two weeks to the day. As the hot water ran over my head, I got the sick feeling that they would stay with me until they married me off to Bob Oliveras or until Ivana Trump threw a Tupperware party, whichever came first. Of course, in actuality, both events had about the same chance of happening; I was beginning to think that the whole painters-in-the-house routine was just some elaborate ploy my great-aunts had devised so that they could legitimately be on hand to drive me nuts.

By the time I went out to the kitchen, I'd abandoned such thoughts and was ready to face the day, which I fully planned on using to paint the house. There was a section in the back that needed a new coat of gray paint, and for once I had no wedding to contemplate, worry about, or attend. I wondered if the Miltons had found Carla's wedding ring yet, and I also wondered if Johnny Page had come to the house last night.

I found both great-aunts in the kitchen, staring at the strangely built black cat as she hovered over a bowl of crunchy cat food without touching it. They looked up and smiled at me and said nothing about Johnny, which more or less proved he hadn't woken them up at midnight.

"Something is wrong with Coal Button," Prudence said.

"She's acting funny," Daisy added.

I poured a cup of coffee and said, "How?"

"Well, she's not eating, for one thing. And she won't let me touch her. Isn't that right, Daisy?"

"That's right. And I can hardly ever get her to leave that area under your couch."

"Wait a moment," I said. "Did you say Coal Button is a she?"

"Of course. Didn't you know?"

"No. You never call her anything but her name. In fact, you rarely even call her that."

"Well, it's true, she is easy to ignore because she's

so quiet, but you have to admit there's been quite a lot going on around here the last few days.''

I got down on my hands and knees in front of the cat, who watched me with suspicious yellow eyes but for once didn't dart away. Gently I reached out and stroked her head, and when she seemed comfortable with that, I ran my hand down along her back and sides. The cat felt big and lumpy. "I'm no expert, but I think Coal Button is going to have kittens," I said.

Daisy giggled. "Nonsense."

"We never let her outside," Prue added.

"What about Mr. Phibbs?" I asked.

Both ladies acted as though I'd suggested the very worst kind of incest. "Mr. Phibbs was . . . decommissioned . . . when I got him," Prudence said awkwardly.

"You mean neutered? Are you sure?"

"Quite," Prudence insisted.

"I still think she's pregnant," I said. In fact, now that I thought about it, I was dumbfounded that I hadn't thought of it a lot earlier.

"Should she see Dr. Stewart?" Prudence asked. "I mean, in case Kylie is right?"

"Prue," Daisy said, shaking her pink head, "we aren't speaking with Dr. Stewart."

"But he's Coal Button's veterinarian," she complained.

"Yes, I know, dear, but are you forgetting what happened to Mr. Fu?"

"Dr. Stewart was sick that night, Daisy. If he'd been well, he would have been there—"

"Now wait a second," I interrupted as I pushed myself to my feet. "I've had about enough of your blaming Theo for Mr. Fu's death. I was there. I saw the care and skill he extended. Mr. Fu couldn't have been in more capable hands, and I find it offensive for you two to suggest that he was somehow responsible for a death he couldn't possibly have prevented."

"But—"

"But nothing," I said so loudly that Coal Button waddled off into the living room. "You didn't want to go with me because it upset you too much, and I understand that, but it means you weren't there making decisions, either. Like I said, I saw him. He knew what he was doing. He stayed on until the end and it was late, and we'd called him away from a social event, but he came and he stayed. And you haven't thanked him or anything. You've just called him names in front of the whole town and accused him of murder. I think it's pretty darn shameful!"

It was the first time in two weeks that my great-aunts both actually seemed to have listened to me. I saw their glances cross; then they both looked down at their hands. I'd balled my fists up by my side as I ranted and raved, and I made them relax now. I didn't know what had come over me, yelling at these two old ladies, defending Theo, but I somehow felt better.

"I don't know what got into me," I said at last.

Prudence looked at Daisy. "Kylie has made a valid point," she said.

Daisy asked, "Prue, could I have been wrong?"

"Perhaps we were both too anxious to blame Mr. Fu's death on someone else," she said softly.

Daisy nodded. "What shall we do now?"

Prudence smiled. "We'll have Kylie take Coal Button and us to see Dr. Brighton."

"We'll apologize!" Daisy said.

"But I have to work tomorrow," I mumbled, relieved I had a legitimate excuse to avoid facing Theo quite yet. I was still remembering our kisses and my conversation with myself in the shower.

Daisy's expression was determined. "Then we'll think of something else."

I escaped out the back door to the tranquility of my paint.

With some trepidation I went to work Monday morning. Trepidation on two counts. One, I was a little concerned about what plans my great-aunts would come up with to apologize to Theo and Dr. Stewart. Two, I was more than a little concerned that there would be a firing squad waiting for me at Barton's.

It was a valid concern. I was early, but Mrs. Sullivan was earlier, and she called me into her office.

Mrs. Sullivan was about a hundred years old. She made my great-aunts seem like tender young sprouts. Of course, she wasn't really that old, but she had the heavily wrinkled skin of a heavy smoker and the deep, gravelly voice to match. Since she never smoked in front of her employees, meetings with her tended to be rather abrupt as she had to sandwich them in between nicotine fits.

A small woman with salt-and-pepper hair and a penchant for black knit suits, Mrs. Sullivan sat erect in her chair and tapped a pencil against my personnel file. She was staring at a paper filled with all sorts of interesting things about me. At least, I presumed that's what the paper was filled with. She took away any lingering doubt after she cleared her throat, which led to a short bout of smoker's cough.

"Now then," she said at last. "Miss Armstrong, I hear you aren't happy here at Barton's."

Gee, I wonder where you heard that? I thought to myself. I said, "Has my performance been poor?"

She wasn't going to be manipulated by me. "I'll just go through this point by point," she said. "You've been late several times in the last two weeks—"

"Twice?"

"Yes. And you've been overheard saying that you don't like weddings or, even more inexcusable, that you don't like Barton's."

"It didn't happen exactly like that—"

"I can understand your bitterness about weddings, at least at first I could, because you yourself were stood up at the altar and it takes a while to get over something like that, but enough time has passed for you to have put it behind you. But bad-mouthing Barton's—''

"I may not be enchanted with weddings, Mrs. Sullivan, but I do like the women who come in here." Well, most of them, I amended privately. There was the Nightmare Bride, but I wisely decided to skip over her. "I want what is best for them," I added. "I try to—"

"Furthermore, you've ignored good-paying customers, flirted while on the job, and, most important, I suppose, given extremely poor advice to a Barton's bride."

"Such as?" I inquired.

"Such as suggesting a dog carry a twenty-thousand-dollar wedding ring, which I would also like to inform you is still lost and may never be found."

"That's a shame." For some perverse reason I felt like laughing. I had a feeling I was tiptoeing around hysteria. "Everything you've said is a half-truth. There's another side. Will you let me tell it to you?"

"Are you calling Mrs. Harry Milton a liar?"

"Not exactly."

"She is one of our very best customers. The Milton wedding brought well over ten thousand dollars into this store."

"But I alone did not make the decision to have Kipper carry the ring."

"That is not what Mrs. Milton said. Now, Miss Armstrong, if it were just this, but on top of these other charges and along with your poor attitude toward weddings, let alone Barton's itself, I'm afraid I'm going to have to let you go."

It took me a moment to grasp her intent. I finally cried, "You're firing me?"

"I'm terminating your employment. Of course, we'll pay you a week's salary as agreed upon when you came to work, but I would like you to clear your personal belongings out of your desk right away. And please, try to do no further damage to Barton's reputation."

"But who will take care of my appointments today?"

"Mrs. Wilkerson will cover for you. In fact, I believe she will take over the bridal department."

"Well," I said, not surprised but definitely betrayed, "what I should do now is wish you good luck, because with Madge at the helm, you're going to need it. You'll forgive me if I don't."

I saw her hands fumble with a bulge in her jacket pocket, which I took to be a package of cigarettes. She cleared her throat and said, "That will be all, Miss Armstrong."

I heard the click of her lighter as I closed the door behind myself.

Madge refused to meet my eyes as I passed her. I went to my desk, opened the drawer, and looked at the measly assortment of personal items I'd collected over the last four years. I took a shopping bag from under the counter, dumped my drawer into it, and looked over at Madge.

She looked away. I knew she could hardly wait to get over to my department. Unable to leave my brides as up in the air as Barton's had just left me, I took my appointment book over to Madge and plopped it down in front of her.

"The gowns for the Garvey wedding need to be ordered today. Michelle Green's dress is up in alterations; you need to call and see if it's ready for her. A shipment of formal wear is due to arrive in about two hours, and you need to have most of it out here as soon as possible because we're running low. The Night— . . . I mean, Fiona Catalina . . . is due this afternoon." I paused for a second and added, "She's a darling, sweet as the day is long. She loves lace and satin and pretty little bows. You'll love her. She's a pussycat."

Madge looked at me strangely, so I stopped before I gave myself away. "Anyway, these other notations are clear."

"You're being awfully decent about this," Madge said.

"No, I'm not." I smiled and turned away from her.

What does the rest of the world do on a Monday morning? I wondered as I drove aimlessly around town. I dreaded going home and telling my great-aunts what had happened. The more I thought about it, the more I decided what I really needed was a sympathetic shoulder to cry on, and what's a mother for if not that?

I drove past her store to see if the lights were on. As it was closed on Mondays, I didn't expect she'd be there except that once in a while she went in and organized things when there weren't a dozen chattering patrons asking her advice about how to iron on decals, or make a dried-flower wreath, or tole paint a decorative birdhouse. The lights were off and the Closed sign was firmly in place, so I drove over to her house.

It was about ten o'clock by the time I pulled into her driveway and parked beside her van. I noticed a red car parked in front of the house, but since she was always complaining about the neighbors cluttering *her* curb with *their* car, I didn't pay it much attention.

Mother saw me as I walked along her sidewalk. She was standing at the sink washing dishes, and though she smiled, I saw her look over her shoulder. I was at the sliding-glass door by then, and I saw a man get up from the table and walk into the shadows of the house.

Yikes. She'd said something about dating other men, and here she was, apparently throwing a brunch for one of them, and I'd blundered in uninvited and unannounced. Embarrassed but knowing it was too late to retreat without saying something, I tapped on the glass and opened the door.

"Kylie," Mother said, again looking over her shoulder.

"I'm sorry, Mom. I didn't know you had company. I'll call you later."

I hadn't taken a step inside, but she came over to the door and frowned at me. She was wearing a very pretty flowered dress and sandals, and her eyes were bright. I thought she looked lovely.

"What are you doing away from work? Is something wrong with Prudence or Daisy—"

"No, nothing like that. I'll talk to you later."

"Something is wrong, isn't it?" she said, using her mother's intuition. Either that or I looked as miserable as I felt.

"It's nothing. . . ."

"What is it?" she demanded. She pulled on my hand, and I came in as far as the table. There was an almost-empty plate on the table where the man had been sitting. He didn't eat the crusts on his bread.

"Kylie?"

I sighed and said, "I lost my job."

"Oh, no."

"Yes. I got canned, fired, ousted. And the reasons were all trumped up, except for the part where the dog carried Carla's wedding ring off toward the eighteenth hole. I have to share responsibility for that."

"This is going to take a little while, isn't it?" she asked, and once again, her head twisted backward, toward the living room, where the man I'd glimpsed through the sliding-glass door had retreated.

"Yes. That's why I'll call you later or you call me when you're . . . available."

"I'm always available to talk to you," she said, her gaze back on me.

I touched her cheek. "I know, Mom. But this isn't the right time." I gestured toward the half-eaten meal and added, "I'm a big girl. I shouldn't have come running to you." Before she could protest, I left.

I drove home because I couldn't think of anything else to do. I shouldn't have worried about my great-aunts making a fuss about my arriving home unexpectedly in the middle of the morning, because from the moment I walked through door, they thought only of my homecoming and not the reasons behind it.

"How wonderful!" Daisy exclaimed. "Prue, Kylie is home. Call and cancel that cab."

"Why are you so glad to see me?" I asked Daisy as she pinned a small black hat on her head.

"Because we won't have to take a cab, dear. Prue always becomes so upset when they overcharge us. It's become something of an embarrassment. Don't tell her I said that."

"I promise," I said, and though it's crazy, I began to feel a little more lighthearted. It was as though I'd entered an alternate universe, one with its own rules and forces I couldn't comprehend but might as well go along with. I temporarily forgot about my job and Johnny and Theo and just settled back to see what my great-aunts had planned.

"Prue," Daisy repeated, her voice at full force, "we're going to be late."

"Where are we going?" I asked, but of course I knew. Given the day I'd already had, where else would we be going? And somehow that was okay too; I even began to suspect that I was looking forward to it.

"To see Dr. Brighton, of course," she confirmed my suspicion. "By the way, Bob called this morning. I invited him to dinner tomorrow night."

This was different! "Daisy—"

"Don't fuss, dear. It's unbecoming. Prue, honestly—"

Just then, Great-Aunt Prudence appeared. She had put Coal Button in the carrying case. It would be an understatement to say that the cat was unimpressed with this plan. She crouched in the corner of the cage, emitting a pitiful meow every few seconds.

Prudence had put on her blue dress, the one she'd worn to Matt's wedding. She'd added a white hat and white gloves. "Kylie," she said, "it's so kind of you to take time off from work to help us. Isn't that right, Daisy?"

"That's right," Daisy agreed. "Kylie, you won't get in trouble for it, will you, dear?"

"No one will care a whit," I told her truthfully.

Daisy pinched my cheek. I felt like Alice must have felt when she fell through the looking glass. "Let's go," I said.

* * *

"Kylie is right—Coal Button is pregnant." Theo struggled to keep his mouth from breaking into a grin and added, "She's very pregnant, within days of delivering."

"Kittens," Daisy said softly, reverently, and I knew we were all thinking how delightful it was that new life should follow death so closely. I was thinking something else as well. I was thinking that I loved Theo Brighton and didn't want him to give up on me as he threatened to the night before. For his part, Theo was acting as though I were as noticeable as an extra tongue depressor.

Prudence got a pad of paper and a pencil out of her purse. "Now," she said officially, "what exactly are we to do?"

He was shining a light into Coal Button's yellow eyes, and he finished looking before he answered my great-aunt. As he gently palpated Coal Button's distended middle, he said, "You said she likes to stay under the sofa?"

"That's right, but now that she is about to become a mother, we'll have to encourage her to pick a better spot. The kitchen, perhaps—"

Theo interrupted. "What you do is go home and put an old towel in a nice shallow box, and then you put the box right under the couch, right where she likes it. She's already chosen her 'nest,' and whether you like it or not, undoubtedly that's where she'll deliver her babies. It's enclosed; she feels safe there. I've taken her temperature; it hasn't dropped yet, which probably means she won't deliver tonight, but I do think it will be soon."

Coal Button meowed as Theo put her back in her carrying case. "She's in excellent health. I really don't think you'll have any problems."

"But you will attend the birth, won't you?" Daisy asked.

Prudence said, "Of course, you must. We can't risk anything happening to Coal Button."

He'd been washing his hands. When he turned, for the first time that morning, he actually looked at me. By now I was used to the THUMP that accompanied his gaze, but the flutter I felt afterward jolted me. I looked down at my hands as he said, "You call me when it starts, and if it's humanly possible, I'll come."

"But how will we know when it starts?" Daisy pleaded.

"It will begin with a loss of water, which will be followed within a half hour or so by the birth of the first kitten. You'll know. But I must warn you, ladies, that cats seem to always give birth in the dead of night, and you might very well wake up one morning to a litter of kittens."

"Coal Button wouldn't do that to us, would you, Coal Button?" Daisy crooned.

Coal Button, sensing her moment in the spotlight, meowed on cue.

Theo laughed. He said, "I'll have the office give you some vitamins for the cat. Meanwhile, try to leave her alone. Coal Button will know what to do even though this is her first litter. And after the kittens are weaned, you might want to consider having her spayed so there won't be any additional 'surprises.'"

Prudence, turning bright red, mumbled, "Yes, of course. There are enough kittens in the world."

Daisy said, "But I'm kind of glad, considering that we just lost Mr. Fu, that Coal Button is going to have babies. Can you tell what color they're going to be?"

This stumped Theo. He finally laughed softly and answered, "There is probably a good chance that at least one of them will be black, but with kittens and puppies, one never knows."

Prudence swallowed and said, "Doctor, this is an indelicate question, and I hope you'll forgive me, but I have been worrying about it ever since Kylie said Coal Button might be having babies." She paused, apparently struggling to find the right words.

Theo said, "Come now, Prudence, you can ask your pet's doctor anything, right?"

"I hope so," she blurted out. She took a deep breath and then, in a rush of words that almost ran together, she said, "I've been worrying about all the stuff, blood and things, that comes out with a baby. I mean, I assume it comes out. What happens to it? Must Daisy and I clean it up?"

Theo put his hands on the examining table and leaned

toward her. His face very somber, he said, "That's what I meant about Coal Button knowing what to do. She'll ingest all that 'stuff.' In fact, it's very important that she do so because it contains hormones that stimulate lactation and calcium that will help prevent eclampsia."

"Eclampsia?" both great-aunts repeated as one.

"Convulsions due to lack of calcium. So you can see how important it is to let Mother Nature guide Coal Button."

"But what if she suffers from this eclampsia, anyway?" Prudence asked, gasping.

I looked up at Theo. He didn't know my great-aunts as well as I did. Unwittingly, he'd given them something else to worry about, but he covered his bases by saying, "In the extremely unlikely case that happens, and I stress the word extremely, I would administer a very small dose of calcium intravenously. Now, is there anything else I can do for you ladies?"

Prudence shot a pointed look at Daisy, who sighed heavily and said, "Just one more thing, Doctor. We'd . . . I'd . . . like to thank you for trying to save Mr. Fu. I'd also like to tell you how sorry I am that I was so nasty to you. I will not offer any excuses, but as my grand-niece pointed out so . . . vocally . . . I do owe you an apology. Will you accept it?"

Theo endeared himself forever to these two women as he reached out and covered Daisy's hand with his own. "Of course, and I do thank you. But please, you mustn't concern yourself with this for another moment. I'm a veterinarian, and I understand how devastating these things can be, but now we can all look forward to greeting Coal Button's family, can't we?''

Prudence nodded. ''That's right. Now we must find Dr. Stewart and apologize to him—''

''That won't be necessary,'' Theo started to say, but Prudence stilled him with a withering glance.

''Of course it's necessary, young man. Come along, Daisy.''

As my great-aunts gathered up their purses and the cat, Theo and I stared at each other. I was remembering the feel of his lips on mine, the tender strength of his hands. I was also remembering the implication of the words he'd spoken. He'd told me to find out how I really felt about Johnny Page because it was getting in the way of his pursuit of the future. Did that mean he wanted to pursue a future with me?

How had this happened? How had I gone from a member in good standing with the ''I-will-never-love-again'' crowd to this blithering idiot about to faint with the intensity of my emotions? It was absolutely amazing to me, but I could hardly remember how intensely I'd felt about not dating men. Had I actually thought I could resist a man like Theo Brighton forever? Why had I wanted to? Because I'd been hurt? Who hasn't?

''I don't need to talk to Johnny Page,'' I said as my great-aunts bustled out the door.

"Yes, you do," he said.

"No—"

"You can't abandon everything overnight," he interrupted. "You have to give yourself time."

"When all I can think about is kissing you?" I asked softly.

"Especially then. That's chemistry, remember?"

"And you want more?"

"I want everything. Everything," he repeated, emphasizing the word. "Two days ago you were never going to fall in love again, never going to marry, never going to have children. You were going to live alone forever. And in the back of your heart I suspect you were waiting for Johnny to realize what he'd abandoned and come back. And now he has, and all of a sudden you're ready to throw yourself at me."

"How nicely you put it!" I said dryly.

"It's costing me; trust me. I think you know what I'd rather do."

Again we stared at each other until finally I whispered, "Theo, I've put down the drawbridge."

"Then take a moment to walk outside and feel the sun on your face," he said equally softly. "And find Johnny."

"And after I do, are you still going to send me packing? Are you going to give up on me, Theo?"

He opened his mouth, but before he could speak,

Prudence stuck her head in the door and said, "Kylie? There you are. We've settled everything with Dr. Stewart. Come along, child, it's time we get Coal Button back under the couch."

Chapter Eight

*C*oal Button crouched in her box. I thought I heard her make a sound, so I got down on my hands and knees and peered at her, waiting to see if it happened again. It did. I listened very hard and finally identified it as a purr.

"Well, I'll be!" I told her as I stroked her sleek head, the only part of her that was sleek. "You're welcome," I added as the sound grew louder.

It finally occurred to Prudence that it was after lunch and I still hadn't gone back to work. She took me aside so Daisy couldn't hear us and said, "You didn't really come home from work to take us to the vet, did you?"

I shook my head. "I was fired this morning."

Her shock was palpable. "No!"

"I'm afraid so."

She leaned very close and asked, "Did you steal something?"

"Of course not," I replied gently. "I hope you know me better than that."

"Of course I do, but one must ask. I learned something from Dr. Brighton this morning. One should strive to get things out in the open."

I nodded agreement.

"Then what did you do?" Prudence asked.

Sighing, I said, "I really don't know. A lot of little things, I guess. Silly things that weren't really wrong but, taken out of context, made me look bad. Listen, I really don't want to talk about this—"

"Don't tell Daisy," Prudence said, "but a few years ago a dear old friend of mine passed away. A gentleman friend," she added with a twinkle in her eye. "He left me a small endowment that I've had no cause to use. I want you to have it."

"Oh, Aunt Prudence, I couldn't—"

"But you must! You're my grand-niece, and I won't have you turning into a bag lady."

I swallowed a smile. Here was a woman who short-changed cab drivers and bought chicken wings on sale, and she was offering me her small inheritance. "I have some money put away too," I told her. "There are other jobs; I'll find something."

She nodded. "That's the spirit. And that nice Bob Oliveras is still interested in you too. If you married him—"

"I'm not going to marry Bob Oliveras," I told her firmly.

She clicked her tongue. "Perhaps. Well, since the painters called early this morning and told us there's been another delay, at least you won't have to face this unpleasantness alone. Daisy and I will be with you for at least another week."

I tried to look pleased, but my first reaction was frustration. My second reaction was humor, and I'm afraid I giggled, laughed, and chuckled until tears rolled down my cheeks.

"Whatever are you carrying on about?" Prudence demanded.

"Life," I said, "and swarming locusts."

She shook her head. "I'm worried about you, Kylie. You've been acting strange today."

"Yes," I agreed. "I have."

It took me a half a dozen calls to locate Johnny Page, but I finally tracked him down at one of his friends' houses. He came on the line all smooth and silky and apologetic for startling me Saturday night. I asked him if we could meet somewhere out of the way that night, and he suggested a spot that had been one of our favorites, a state park overlooking the ocean. "Bring a jacket," he said, "and we'll stroll along the beach."

I agreed. It would be hard to find a more private spot than a remote beach, and privacy is what I craved. I didn't want to run into anyone I knew; I hoped no one would ever find out that I'd even spoken to the man, because it was a small town and I didn't want to feed the rumor mill. Did the rest of my family think as Theo did, that, like some fairy-tale princess in need of a kiss, I'd been waiting for Johnny to return? Certainly my mother had. I needed to find out the truth, but I didn't want an audience.

I wasn't sure what to wear to a meeting with a former fiancé, but in the end settled on jeans and a warm sweater, as the evenings were cold along the water. I left my great-aunts sitting on two chairs facing the sofa. Mr. Phibbs sat on the back of Prudence's chair, and Coal Button lay in her box, trying to ignore all the attention.

The parking lot was deserted, which meant that Johnny wasn't there yet, and I was fifteen minutes late. I sat in the car for another fifteen, and then a late-model truck rolled up and Johnny emerged. I got out of my car; it crossed my mind that to an onlooker we must appear like two spies about to exchange secret information.

"I was surprised you called," he said. "After the way you bolted the other night—"

"Shall we walk?" I asked.

He led the way down the path toward the beach. I stared at the back of his head as we descended, reminding myself that I had to find out how I really felt and the only way to do that was to be completely honest with myself. That wasn't going to be as easy as it might sound, as it meant that I would have to expose myself to the possibility of rejection. I'd have to risk my pride, and since pride had been what had kept me going for so long, I wasn't sure what I would do without it. But if I didn't find out, I risked losing something far more precious.

Once we gained the beach, we both turned south and made our way across the dunes toward the water. For quite a while we walked silently. At last Johnny said, "I've missed the ocean."

"Where have you and Donna been all this time?" Donna was Johnny's brother's wife, or at least she had been. I had no idea what condition that marriage was currently in.

"We went to Mexico," he said. "Cabo, at least for a while. Donna got homesick right away, and I got bored with her, and then she split. I moved back to the States, went to Texas, where I have an uncle with a cattle ranch. I've been playing cowboy for a while."

"Sounds interesting."

"Are you still working at Barton's?"

"No," I said without elaborating.

"I thought Carla said—"

"It's a long story," I interrupted, and he dropped it.

We climbed over a big piece of driftwood. Johnny helped me down the far side and kept my hand in his. He guided me to another large beached log and sat down on the sand with his back against the wood, pulling me down to sit beside him.

"I've missed you too, Kylie," he said.

He was looking into my eyes. It was so strange sitting close to him. If he hadn't run off, we'd be two years married by now, maybe even have a child. So much would be between us.

"Tell me exactly why you left," I said because I'd sworn to myself I was going to open the Johnny Page file and kick out all the ghosts.

He put his hand against my cheek. The wind blew cool, and his hand was warm. He cupped my chin and asked, "Why delve into the past? Let's look ahead to the future."

"No," I told him. "I have to have a few answers. Why did you leave?"

His hand fell down into his lap. He looked out toward the ocean and finally said, "I got cold feet. Right on the eve of our wedding, I really thought about being married, and I got scared. It wasn't you; it was the commitment. I knew I couldn't go through with it."

"You knew the night before?"

He nodded. "Yeah. I should have called you, I know. But I buried myself in Donna instead. I was a rat." He looked up at me and blinked his eyes. "But I'm back. I've heard from people how hurt you were, how you drew into yourself once I was gone. I feel really bad about that, Kylie. I want to make it up to you. I'm older now, more stable. Let's start over again."

As he'd been speaking, he'd moved closer and closer until his lips were almost on top of mine. Now he touched my lips with his, wrapped an arm around my back, and pulled me close. I tried with all my heart to feel something—everything—anything in that kiss, but all I could think of was the fact that he apparently had a hangnail and it was catching on my sweater.

When the kiss was over, he stared into my eyes. I had no idea what he was thinking; I wondered if I'd ever known what he was thinking. I could barely remember loving him. In fact, my most vivid memory of him centered on the one thing he hadn't done— namely, show up at the church.

"What are you thinking, Kylie?" he asked.

I smiled as a sea gull landed a few yards away. "I'm thinking that I'm in love in a way I've never been in love before, and I owe it all to you."

He grinned and, raising my hand to his lips, kissed my knuckles.

"If I'd married you," I continued, "I wouldn't be free right now. We'd probably have a cat or a dog, and I'd probably, at some time, have to take the animal to the new veterinarian in town. I'd think he was fascinating and gorgeous, and he'd think the same things about me, but we'd both be too decent to do anything about it. In the end I'd come home with the dog or the cat—home to you—and it wouldn't be a castle with lilies in the moat, it would just be a house. I'm very happy and very grateful that you spared me that life, that you left me free to really find my heart. Thank you, Johnny."

"I don't understand—"

"Yes, you do. You've always understood our relationship better than I have. Maybe I made it into what I wanted it to be without consideration of you."

"But I'm the one who left. Is this your way of getting back at me? Dragging me all the way out here and then rejecting me?"

I thought for a second because I wanted the answer to be truthful, for my sake as well as his. At last I said, "No. I needed some answers, and you gave them to me. Like I said, I owe you a lot, and I'll always be grateful you had the good sense to save me from myself."

"You've gotten strange," he grumbled.

I laughed. The sudden noise startled the sea gull and it flew off over the ocean. "I've heard that more than once today." I stood up, sighed, and brushed the sand off my pants. "Are you coming? I have someone to see yet tonight."

"Obviously another man," Johnny said as he stood.

"No, as a matter of fact. I want to see my mother."

He shook his head, and side by side we started back to the parking lot.

The red car was nowhere to be seen, so I felt pretty safe knocking on the front door. I chose this door instead of the sliding-glass door because I didn't want to inadvertently see someone she wasn't ready to share with me yet. My mother wasn't up-to-date on the new me, I realized, the me who was twelve hours older than the old me she'd seen this morning, the me who wasn't so positive that marriage might not be worth the risk, the me who thought that true love was an honorable and achievable goal.

Mostly, I wanted to tell her I'd seen Johnny, because in some way her life and mine had been parallel. True, she'd had twenty years of marriage, and I'd had only a few months' engagement, but we'd both been left unexpectedly, and neither one of us had ever had the opportunity to tell the jerk off. Of course, in the end, I hadn't really told my jerk anything, and that was the beauty of it; that was what I wanted to share. You didn't actually need to say all the words you'd created over the years. They weren't necessary.

She probably knew all of this, but my head was still reeling with the implications. I wanted her to know that I was over being a nondating recluse, that I was sick of licking my wounds, that I had fallen in love with a terrific man whom I wanted her to really meet.

For all those reasons I blundered back into my mother's life without calling ahead. She answered my knock, and the first thing she did was look over her shoulder, back into the house.

"Not again," I cried, smiling. "Talk about timing. I'm very sorry. But this time I wasn't coming to complain. I was coming to tell you how happy I am."

She was still wearing her pretty flowered dress. She said, "What's happened to you? You look one hundred percent different than you did a few hours ago. Did you get your job back?''

''No, not my job, something a lot better. I have officially reclaimed my spirit.''

She shook her head. ''You've started talking in riddles.''

All this time, she'd been holding the door close to her body so that I couldn't see inside. I touched her hand and said, ''It's okay, Mom. I'm out of here. And I promise I won't come over again without calling ahead.''

''It's just that—''

''It's okay. You don't need to explain. But I would love to meet him sometime, when you're ready.''

''She's ready now,'' a deep voice said as a man's hand appeared on the door above my mother's head. The door opened farther until he stood there in full view. For a second I saw a nice-looking guy in his fifties, a guy who resembled my brother Matt. And then it hit me. I was looking at my father.

He looked a little like Matt. His hair was gray at the temples, the color of his eyes, but he had my brother's jaw and straight nose. When I'd been sixteen, I'd entertained fantasies that he'd turn so ugly the secretary would leave him. It hadn't been clear to me then whether I wanted him to return to my mother or just go crawl into a hole in the ground. I just wanted him away from *her*.

He hadn't turned ugly.

"Hello, Kylie," he said softly.

I felt tears running down my cheeks. I didn't know what to say. For ten years I hadn't known if he was alive or dead, and here he was, standing in front of me in the doorway of the house in which I'd grown up, next to the woman who was my mother. For one suspended moment it was as though time had reversed and all was as it once had been. We were three people united by blood, but in a way, at that moment, we were three strangers.

I looked at my mother and found her staring at my father. There was so much emotion in her eyes that it broke what little control I had left.

"How could you have him here?" I asked her as I wiped the tears away.

Her eyes whipped around to me. "Kylie—"

"I mean it, Mother," I said, my voice remote. "How can you stand to have him near you?"

She bit at her lip, looked down at her hands, which she had clasped together so tightly her knuckles were white, and said, "If you understood love, Kylie, you wouldn't have to ask."

I wanted to run away, but something glued the soles of my shoes to the porch. I looked away from my mother's eyes and faced my father.

"I don't know what to say to you," I told him.

He was wearing a pair of jeans and a tan shirt with the sleeves rolled up to just under his elbows. He stuck his hands in his pockets, but before he hid them I saw that they were trembling, and I realized he was as nervous about seeing me as I was about seeing him. He said, "I contacted your mother a few days ago. I asked her if I could come home. She wasn't thrilled with the idea, but she didn't say no, so I took a chance and came."

"Just like that," I said bitterly.

He nodded. His face was slender and somewhat weathered. It suddenly occurred to me that he hadn't had a very easy life lately, and that secretly pleased me.

"You've turned into a beautiful woman," he said. "You look like your mother."

"Why did you come back now?"

He looked at my mother, then back at me. "I came back because I realized I'd made an awful mistake. Actually, I realized it right away, but I was proud . . . and stubborn."

"So you figure you can waltz into our lives and turn back the clock?"

"No—"

"Then why now? Why not five years ago? Why not yesterday? Why not five years from now?"

"I knew Matt was getting married, but I didn't want to show up before that and perhaps ruin things for him."

"How considerate of you!"

My mother snapped, "Kylie—"

"Let her speak," my father said.

"We didn't know where you were, if you were alive. You never called. Ten Christmases, ten birthdays, ten years, Dad. Ten long years."

"I know. I lost them too. And I don't expect you to forgive me, not now, not ever."

"But I have," my mother said softly, and it dawned on me that forgiving a man you loved might be easier than forgiving a parent.

"So you're here to stay?" I asked at last.

"If she'll have me."

I looked at my mother, who was once again gazing up at my father, and I knew that one way or another, somehow or other, I was going to have to find a way back to him, or I would lose her too. I said, "Welcome home, Dad," and I didn't know if I meant it or not.

I tried calling Theo that night but wasn't too upset when he failed to answer his phone. Finding my long-lost father had put a little bit of a tailspin on my euphoria. So I sat on the floor and stared at Coal Button for a while, but as she seemed in no hurry to enter the state of motherhood, I finally took myself to bed.

The next morning, as I was perusing the Help Wanted ads, Daisy sat down next to me. "I know you lost your job, dear. Prue told me. Now, I have a secret to tell you that is just between the two of us. Promise."

I folded the newspaper over on itself and said, "Okay, I promise."

"You know we live on our father's annuity, but what Prue doesn't know is that I have a little extra money set aside. I had a job a few years ago. Prue thought it was volunteer work, because I'm afraid that is what I led her to believe. Anyway, the money is just sitting in the bank, and I want you to have it to tide you over this difficult period."

As I stared into her eyes, I wondered how I had let these two women become such faint relations. For years I'd more or less ignored their existence, and yet each of them had offered me the money she held dear enough to keep secret from the other when she saw that I might be in trouble. I hastened to assure Daisy that not only did I plan on being reemployed within the week, but also that I had savings of my own for just such an emergency. She told me to tell her if the situation changed; then she went back to the living room as it was her turn to keep an eye on Coal Button.

Not long after she left the kitchen, I heard a light tapping on the back door. I got up, opened the door, and found my mother.

"May I come in?" she asked me.

"Of course." I sat back down at the table. Mom paced for a few moments; I noticed she stayed away from the connecting door to the living room, where Daisy could be heard offering words of encouragement to Coal Button.

"I don't want them to know I'm here," she whispered. "I don't think they like me anymore."

"Of course they like you," I said, though I agreed with her. "Stop pacing and sit down. May I get you something to drink—"

"No, no, nothing. I just didn't want things to stay the way they were last night when you left my house. I want to try to make you understand—"

"This isn't necessary—"

"It is for me. You're my daughter. You've stood by me for the last ten years, and you've suffered. I know you have. Oh, it was hard on Matt, but he was twenty and already out on his own when your father left. It was different for you."

For an instant I was back to being sixteen, lying awake at night as Mom cried herself to sleep in her bedroom, muffling the noise in her pillow so that I wouldn't hear, but I had. I said, "I guess that's all in the past."

She finally sat down. "The past. It never goes away, Kylie. We think we tame it, we think we put it in its place, and then. . . . When your father called and asked about coming to see me, I was scared. I thought I'd relegated him into the closet along with our wedding china and the sterling tea service I've never used. Finally I told him to come, because I'd been pressuring you to face your past, and here I was with an opportunity to face mine.

"I knew he was coming for days, and during that time I rehearsed everything I've always wanted to say to him. You know how it is—you wake up in the middle of the night with another point to make or another angry remark to snarl and he's not there, so you stuff it back inside. I dug it all out and got it ready to throw at him. And then he was there, and he was crying, and he was apologizing, and all the anger and all the hurt didn't seem so important anymore. Not that I didn't say a few choice words, but the fact of the matter is that I've never stopped loving the man, and if there is a way to rebuild what we once had, I want to take it.''

She stood again. We were both crying. She took a couple of paper towels off the roll and handed me one, and for a few seconds we wiped our faces and blew our noses. Then she said, ''I know I'm a fool. I know what everyone will say about me. I just don't care.''

''I understand,'' I said softly. ''You're right—people will talk, but so what? They talked when he left, and you survived that. At least this time he'll be there to help you through it. That's my only concern, that if you give your heart, he realizes the value of the gesture and doesn't hurt you again.''

''I don't believe he will purposely hurt me again,'' she said. ''But there are no guarantees. And we're going to take it slowly, one day at a time. Maybe too much time has passed. Maybe it's too late.''

''But you have to find out.''

She nodded. She blew her nose again and reached down and hugged me. ''I didn't expect you to be so reasonable about this.''

I patted her hand. ''He's just lucky he came back

when he did. He's reaping the benefit of the new, wiser me.''

''Will you tell me about it?'' she asked.

''Later. You have a lot on your mind right now, and I think I'd like to discuss things with Theo before I say more.''

''Theo? The vet? The cute one?''

I smiled. ''That about sums him up, all right.''

Just then Daisy cleared her throat. When we both looked around at her, she waltzed dramatically into the kitchen, drew herself a glass of water, downed a sip of it, put the glass in the sink, and, ignoring my mother but smiling at me, waltzed back out.

''Hello, Daisy,'' my mother called.

Daisy came back to the door and said, ''Oh, it's you. I suppose you came to gloat over my little dog's untimely demise.''

''Of course not. I was terribly upset to hear about Mr. Fu's death.''

''You hated the little dear,'' Daisy said.

Mother nodded. ''I'm afraid I wasn't fond of him, that's true. But I am terribly fond of you, so, you see, that accounts for my sorrow.''

Daisy seemed stunned by this tender revelation.

My mother asked, ''Is Prue here? I'd like to take both of you out to dinner tonight. I'd like us to be friends again.''

Daisy sniffed and said, ''We are having a dinner guest tonight, a young man who is very fond of your daughter, though she informs me she does not date. However, I heard her planning a clandestine meeting on the phone with that Johnny Page, and there's our vet who seems quite smitten with her. For a girl who doesn't date, our Kylie seems to have an inordinate number of men around, but I'm banking that Bob will win out in the end.''

My mother and I exchanged bemused glances.

Prudence walked through the back door right then. When she saw my mother and Daisy facing each other, she said, ''Now, ladies, please, set a good example for the child.''

As she put her bag of groceries on the counter, I realized I was the child she was referring to. I smiled again.

Daisy said, ''*She* came over here to apologize and to invite us out to dinner, but I told her Bob is coming—''

''How about tomorrow night?'' Prudence asked.

My mother stammered, ''Sure . . . tomorrow, that's fine.''

''Never pass up a free meal,'' Prudence told her sister as she began unpacking the bag.

Chapter Nine

''*C*hicken wings,'' Bob said. ''I had no idea there were so many chicken-wing recipes in the world.''

Daisy leaned across the table and confided, ''Prue has dozens of them.''

''And Daisy is a wonder in the kitchen,'' Prudence said, returning the compliment. I saw from the corner of my eye that Bob was picking at the glob on his plate.

Where was Theo? I'd tried calling him several times that night. There was so much to tell him, so much had happened, but he wasn't at his house, and he wasn't at the office, and all the receptionist would tell me was that he'd taken the day off to attend to personal business.

Eventually, dinner over, we all moved into the living room, where we positioned ourselves so that we could stare at Coal Button. She'd been acting strange all afternoon, and I know all three of us thought that to-night would be the night for the big event. I felt sorry for Bob as we silently engaged in this less than stimulating activity.

"Would you like to go outside?" I asked, pity winning over my determination to stay by Coal Button.

"Yes," he blurted out as he stood. He seemed to remember his manners then and, looking at Daisy and Prudence, thanked them for a wonderful dinner. They accepted his compliments and told him that when I got married, they would be sure to send me on my way with a copy of the recipes.

We both hit the porch laughing. It was dark by now, and I sat down on the cement step under the bug-repellent light. Bob sat beside me.

"There's too much light for what I had planned," he said.

I laughed and didn't respond.

He added, "You don't want me to kiss you, do you?"

"No," I admitted. "I'm sorry—"

"That's okay. You seem different, Kylie."

"A lot has happened in the past few days."

"But you haven't changed your feelings about men, have you?"

"Yes, as a matter of fact, I have."

"Then just not about me."

"No."

"That big, handsome veterinarian?"

I nodded. "Are you really upset, Bob?"

"A little disappointed. You're pretty and smart and funny, and I've enjoyed being around you and your aunts. But you never led me on, so I wasn't really expecting anything."

"At least you'll never have to eat another chicken wing."

He patted my hand. "True."

Within the house, I heard the phone ringing, then Prudence calling out my name. We both stood. "Goodbye, Kylie Armstrong," he said. "Have a good life."

I kissed his cheek and watched him walk down the sidewalk toward his car. My great-aunt yelled my name again.

"This is Kylie," I said into the receiver.

"This is Mrs. Sullivan," a raspy voice said.

"Ah—"

"Yes, well, I'll be short and to the point. I want you to come back to Barton's."

"Why?" I asked.

"Why?"

"Yesterday you fired me; today you want me back. Why?"

She coughed for a few seconds. Finally she said, "Mrs. Wilkerson didn't . . . work out."

"What did Madge do?"

"She told a customer to . . . well, I believe the exact words she said to Miss Catalina are forbidden over the phone."

"I see. The Nightmare Bride got to her, is that right?"

"Nightmare Bride?"

"That's what I silently dubbed Fiona Catalina," I said. "The woman is a royal pain in the neck. If I were you, I wouldn't fire Madge because of her; I'd give her a bonus for ridding Barton's of a pest."

"I didn't fire Madge Wilkerson; she quit. The Garvey party came in today, every last one of them, and changed their minds, wanted a whole new setup. They came while Miss Catalina was there . . . I gather there was quite a commotion. All of them were upset that you weren't there. In fact, Miss Garvey has threatened to pull her business entirely from Barton's. Anyway, it was too much for Mrs. Wilkerson."

"I wish I'd been there," I said, somehow relieved to hear that Mrs. Sullivan was not suffering from a fit of remorse in having unfairly fired me but was acting purely with a business motive. She wanted the Garvey wedding.

"That is exactly the point, Miss Armstrong. So do I."

"But what about the Milton ring?"

"I found out today via the grapevine that the ring was found in a sand trap out near the sixteenth hole. Some golfer found the little pillow, and the ring was still attached. When I called Mrs. Milton to confirm the story, she said that yes, it had been found, that it had been your idea to secure it to the pillow, that it had been her son-in-law's idea to use the dog. I owe you an apology."

"And a ten percent raise?"

There was a moment of silence. "Shall I expect you in the morning?"

"I'll be there," I said just as Daisy burst into the kitchen.

"Get off the phone, Kylie! It's started. Coal Button's water broke!"

"I have to go," I told Mrs. Sullivan and hung up. As I went to see what I could do to help the cat, Daisy began dialing Theo. I didn't have the heart to tell her he was out of town.

"Wherever could he be?" Prudence said for the fiftieth time.

"I left a message with his service," Daisy said. "Dr. Stewart was out delivering a horse somewhere. You'd think Coal Button's babies would take precedence over a horse."

"Calm down," I told them both. It was up to me to be the cool voice of reason, but truth of the matter was that I was dreadfully disappointed that Theo wasn't there. I'd been so looking forward to sharing this event with him, and, of course, I was still bursting with the joy of discovering I loved him. For two years I'd suffocated my feelings, and now that they were outside the castle gates, Prince Charming had taken it on the lam.

Coal Button, on the other hand, was the most composed about-to-be-mother I'd ever seen. She lay in her box and did nothing.

Finally she began howling, and soon after that a kitten emerged. It took well over an hour, but when all was said and done, Coal Button's family consisted of two black balls of fur (one with white socks) and an orange-and-white striped tabby that looked suspiciously like Mr. Phibbs. Daisy and Prudence and I watched, sitting on our hands to keep from interfering. Coal Button seemed to know exactly what to do, though after the last kitten was born, she appeared exhausted.

The doorbell rang. I jumped up to answer, and there was Theo.

"At last," I said as my heart did its THUMP thing. I wanted to throw myself into his arms, but our moment of mutual speculation and wonder was cut short by another yowl from Coal Button.

"Doctor, hurry!" Prudence cried. "What's wrong with her?"

Theo got down on the floor by the box. We were all crowded around, but while the tiny new kittens mewed for their mother, she seemed disinterested in them.

"Coal Button is a first-time mother," Theo said as he palpated her abdomen. "She's a little frightened by this extraordinary turn of events, and she's tired too. There's another kitten here. We'll have to help her.''

He directed me to massage her belly while he ever so tenderly guided the last kitten out into the world. Our gasps of delight were cut short by the tiny gray kitten's stillness.

"The little darling is dead," Prue cried. "Oh, Daisy—"

"Courage, my dear," Daisy said, grasping her sister's hand. "We still have the other three—"

"Look," Theo said softly. "See the way Coal Button is nosing the little fellow? That means he's not dead; he's asphyxiated." Deftly he reached into the box and pinched the umbilical cord. The kitten cried out and began breathing. Coal Button took care of the rest.

"What a fine family you have, Miss Button!" Theo said to the cat, which made my great-aunts giggle. He looked up at them and said, "I don't believe you'll have any trouble finding homes—"

"Homes!" Prudence said. "You mean give them away?"

"Well—"

"I should say not!" Daisy interrupted. There's one for each of us, one for Kylie, and one for you, Doctor."

"But—"

"You can have the darling little gray one," Prudence said. "I'm going to name him Theo because you saved his life."

"What if he is a she?" Theo asked, finally completing a sentence.

"Then we'll name her Theodora. Now, there will be no more talk of dividing Coal Button's family when she's just now acquired it. She's a new mother; we don't want to upset her."

"Of course," Theo said. "It was thoughtless of me." He said it sincerely, with a glitter in his eyes that I found absolutely charming, and, judging from the giggles that escaped my great-aunts, so did they.

Eventually we put a soft towel, warm from the dryer, into a new box and moved the family to clean quarters. As the kittens nursed, Coal Button closed her eyes, her purr more content now, more assured. Motherhood apparently agreed with her. Mr. Phibbs walked by the box, took one look at all the new competition, and sulked off to the bedroom.

"I'll have to give him a little extra attention tomorrow," Prudence said.

Daisy got slowly to her feet and stared down at me and then at Theo. "I was wrong about Bob Oliveras," she said as she stifled a long yawn. "This young man is better. Come along, Prue. Let the doctor take care of the kittens."

"It has been a stimulating evening," Prudence agreed as Theo helped her to her feet. "You will watch over them for a while and make sure everything is okay?"

"Aunt Prudence—" I began, but Theo cut me short.

"Of course. It's part of the service."

Before she closed her bedroom door, Prudence looked out. "Dr. Brighton? Do you like chicken wings?"

I bit my lip as Theo said, "Love 'em."

She nodded and closed the door. Theo sat back down on the floor, on the other side of the box from me, and gazed at the kittens. With Theo close and the night ahead, I had never in my life been as content and happy as I was at that moment.

"They are so adorable," I said.

"It never ceases to amaze me," Theo said as he gently ran a fingertip down the back of the gray kitten. Upon closer inspection we'd found out it had a white tummy and three white toes and a white tip on its tail.

"I guess the five dogs will now have a cat of their own. They wouldn't hurt it—"

"No. They'll follow it around until it gets big enough to hiss, and then it will rule the roost. Funny, but I've never had a cat before."

"I wonder which one they'll give me," I mused.

I touched the orange one. Theo's hand closed over mine, he raised our hands over the box, and then he stood, pulling me to my feet as well. "Come here," he said as he sat in my good green chair. I plopped down on his lap.

"Where were you today?" I asked. "And last night too? I called and called—"

"Why did you call?" he asked, but he thwarted my

attempt to answer by kissing me. I discovered my heart had gone way past thumping wildly and was now into racing. This was heaven, right here in my little house, right here on Theo's lap.

Finally I said, "I called because I wanted to tell you that the princess talked to the ex-Prince Charming. She even kissed him."

He pulled away a little. "I don't believe I asked you to go around kissing—"

"Now wait a second. You told me to find out about Johnny Page, and that's what I did."

"What did you discover about him?"

"Nothing. But I did discover a few things about myself, all of which I'll tell you over the next fifty or sixty years. The gist of it is that I do not love the man. The good part is that I do love you. A lot. A whole lot. Heaps. Mounds—"

I was interrupted again in the most pleasant way. At last, back on the floor by the box of cats, I said, "So where were you all day?"

He dug into his jeans pocket and withdrew a small black box. "I have another fairy tale," he said.

Smiling, I leaned back against the sofa. "Shoot."

"Once upon a time, about thirty-two years ago, a man who looked a lot like me because he was my father fell in love with a woman who looks nothing like you because you're not related, thank goodness."

"I think you're getting a little off track—"

"Hush, let me finish. I can tell I'll have to lock

you out of the room when I try to tell stories to our children. Where was I? Okay. This man asked this woman to love him and marry him and be his forever. She said yes, and they did. They had a handsome, smart son, me, and a daughter they named Amanda, who was a pain from day one, but that's another story. The sad part is that the woman died a few years ago. She knew she was dying, and before it happened, she called her son into her room. She told him that someday he would love someone the way she was loved and when that day happened, he should present the lucky woman with this.'' His gaze rested on the small box.

''Yesterday, right there in one of the examination rooms, smack dab in the middle of the day, I realized that I'd found that woman. I had a sneaking feeling that she would eventually realize she'd found me as well, so I took a little time off from work, drove down to San Francisco, and retrieved this from the safety deposit box I haven't yet moved up here.''

With this, he handed me the box. I opened it to find a diamond and ruby wedding band. Speechless, I took it from the box. It was engraved inside, and I turned it so the light was better. It said, *Love For Eternity, 7–28–60.*

''There's just enough room to engrave another date,'' he said. ''The sentiment seems appropriate already. It expresses perfectly the way I feel about you.''

"Oh, Theo. . . ."

"Don't cry, Kylie. I know we haven't known each other very long; I know you need some time to make sure this is the real thing for you, but I'd like it if you wore the ring as an engagement ring. I would like to know it was on your hand and that you were willing to consider marrying me."

"Now who's talking too much?" I asked as I slipped the ring on my finger and leaned across Coal Button and her four kittens to kiss the man I loved.

It was a double wedding. Amanda married Mike, who happened to be twenty years older than she and, though attractive, he was not the hunk I'd predicted. I married my Theo, heart racing and thumping and going crazy as his killer smile flashed just for me. Amanda had the beautiful Marie as a bridesmaid. I had Prudence and Daisy, whom I told to wear whatever they wanted. Hence, one side of the wedding looked elegant; the other side looked . . . eccentric. My brother, Matt, was Theo's best man, and my father stood by my mother's side and looked nervous.

All and all, it was a glorious wedding. Theo tried to convince me that at one time I hated the ceremony as well as the idea of marriage, but I think he must have confused me with someone else. A man with five dogs, two cats (Mr. Phibbs, Jr., came with me), and a new wife can't be expected to recall every little thing perfectly. I believe his last words to me as he carried me across the threshold of the new house we bought together were, ''Welcome home, Mrs. Bright-on.''

That's perfect enough.